THE HISTORICAL HAGGADAH

By

Abram Epstein

TFG PRESS

THE HISTORICAL HAGGADAH
Published by TFG
Copyright © 2002 by Abram Epstein

For further information, contact the author at:

HistoricalTorah@aol.com

Book design by The Floating Gallery:
331 West 57th Street, #465, New York, NY 10019
(212) 399-1961   www.thefloatinggallery.com

Printed in the United States of America

Abram Epstein
THE HISTORICAL HAGGADAH

1. Author 2. Title 3. Religion
ISBN 0-9671636-9-2
Library of Congress Control Number 2002103328

This Haggadah is dedicated to my brother, Fred Epstein.

As a world-renowned pioneer in pediatric neurosurgery, he has led a generation of children from the darkness of certain death to the light of complete recovery.

About This Haggadah

Brought to life in **The Historical Haggadah**, pre-slavery Egypt was vibrant with Hebrew ceremony—including a lamb and matzah pilgrimage holiday. (The significance of matzah, a sacred bread which actually originated long before the escape, becomes fully understandable for the first time in this account.)

When slavery occurred, the annual pilgrimage was prohibited and fit men were removed from their homes. Only those too young or too old for physical labor, as well as women, were allowed to remain behind in their city, called Goshen. For several decades they lived their lonely lives more-or-less normally—moving the holiday indoors, never giving up hope the families would be reunited and free. Then came the news. the Pharoh, Ramses II was dead. Times were about to change. Moses, a Hebrew leader in exile, heeded God's command at the Burning Bush, and returned to confront the new Pharoh, demanding freedom for the People....

The Historical Haggadah illuminates the legacy of pre-Exodus Egypt to our own time, enriching our rituals and customs by relating them to Hebrew life before and during enslavement.

A supplementary essay entitled, **Passover: Telling It Like It Was** offers a complete history of the holiday. After a general refresher (*For Starters...*) it provides the re-assessment upon which this Haggadah is based (*From Bitter to Sweet...*).

About The Author

Abram Epstein has served as Director of Education for various synagogues, and actively participated in the Manhattan Educators' Council. His graduate studies at New York's Hagop Kevorkian Center focused on Ancient Near Eastern religions and Biblical Judaism. In addition to **The Historical Haggadah**, he has recently completed a major work, **The Documented Biography of Jesus Before Christianity.** His current adult studies program includes a popular course called "The History Behind The Torah."

Preface

The Historical Haggadah is based on a different version of events than that familiar from our seder tradition. The supplementary discussion, ***Passover: Telling It Like It Was*** provides a fresh background study of the circumstances before and during our enslavement, rendering the Exodus more realistically than prior studies. The seder leader may wish to read it before beginning.

Familiarity with the following historical elements is recommended:

A. Our seder has its roots in a time prior to enslavement, when the Hebrew community living in Egypt made an annual pilgrimage to sacrifice lambs and eat unleavened bread (yes, matzah!) at Mount Horeb, a three-day excursion from Goshen. In those days, the holiday was called, "The Festival of Adonay."

B. After the Hebrews had grown to a sizeable community, perhaps over several centuries, the Pharoh (Ramses II) took the physically fit people as slaves, compelling them to leave their homes. Those who were too young or too old (perhaps under 20 and over 50) comprised a community NOT taken away. They lived in relative prosperity with herds of animals, and vineyards—but they were no longer free to leave Egypt. Confined to Goshen, they could no longer make the pilgrimage to Mount Horeb.

C. Most likely the period of enslavement lasted about 75 years (Ca. 1280-1205 B.C.E.). During that time, the Festival of Adonay was moved indoors. Because the firstborn sons of the families were often gone as slaves, their usual role of officiating over the Festival rituals

1

was conducted by elders and all those who were capable, functioning as a priestly community.

D. When the Ten Plagues began, Moses was returning to Egypt—having learned of the Pharoh's death. He was no longer a "wanted fugitive"—and according to our Torah, was directed by God to offer the new Pharoh (Merenptah) a simple choice: Let My people Go—or else.

E. The washing and dietary precautions which even today characterize Jewish lifestyles likely originated with enslavement. When the Festival of Adonay was moved indoors, the house was kept as pure as a shrine. Eventually, this was the miraculous change that saved the Hebrews from the plagues. With the heightened awareness of disease-causing contamination, ritual purity prevented death from "entering" Hebrew homes. (After the escape, these rituals would be codified as commandments—today called ablution and kosher laws.)

The "NARRATORS" are speaking in the present. The seder leader should be the main narrator.

The "READERS" are from the past, some in ancient Egypt—others our "guests," telling what it was like. (Note: Though the Haggadah is more theatrical in style than is customary, it really is not a play. The voices are an echo of the Torah-as-history, nothing more, nothing less.) With no fixed roles, each participant should feel free to play different characters, including those of young readers if none are present. (On this night 85 years old is still young!)

PART ONE

NARRATOR (Seder leader): As we begin our seder, let us review the evening's traditional order of customs and rituals. While omitting none, our seder shall illuminate their origins and significance.

ALL ARE WELCOME TO SING ALONG:

קַדֵשׁ • וּרְחַץ • כַּרְפַּס • יַחַץ • מַגִּיד • רָחְצָה • מוֹצִיא • מַצָּה •

מָרוֹר • כּוֹרֵךְ • שֻׁלְחָן עוֹרֵךְ • צָפוּן • בָּרֵךְ • הַלֵּל • נִרְצָה •

KADESH . U-RE-CHATZ . KARPAS . YA-CHATS . MA-GEED . RACH-TSA

MOTSIE . MATZAH . MAROR . KO-RAYCH . SHUL-CHAN O-RAYCH

TSA-FOON . BA-RAYCH . HA-LAYL . NEER-TSA

MAKE KIDDUSH
THE SEDER LEADER WASHES HANDS
DIP A GREEN VEGETABLE IN SALT WATER (the first dip)
BREAK THE MIDDLE PIECE OF MATZAH AND HIDE THE AFIKOMEN
TELL THE STORY OF THE EXODUS (illustrated by symbolic foods
on the seder plate, the stack of three matzah, and customary
readings)
Part Two
ALL WASH THEIR HANDS
BRACHA OVER BREAD
BRACHA OVER MATZAH
BRACHA OVER BITTER HERBS (dipped in Charoset, the second dip)
EAT THE MATZAH WITH BITTER HERBS (the "Hillel" sandwich)
EAT DINNER
SHARE IN THE AFIKOMEN
GIVE THANKS FOR OUR FOOD
JOIN IN HALLEL PSALMS OF PRAISE
PRONOUNCE THE REQUIRED RITUALS COMPLETE

NARRATOR (continuing) Now let's imagine we are back in Egypt. It is about 3,500 years ago.

READER: Generations of our families, residing in the Delta city of Goshen have lived well, farming and raising herds of animals such as goats, sheep, lambs, and cows.

Generations earlier our forefather Joseph had achieved influence and was able to invite our families to this prosperous country.

Politically, we have been treated well. Pharohs have come and gone, and we have been permitted freedom to come and go as well.

Anyway, in a few hours we will have finished packing for the three-day excursion, our annual pilgrimage to Horeb mountain. It is the tenth of Nisan, and we have selected our animals. They are firstlings, young animals that will be perfect for the sacrifice—and for food. It's not everyday that we get to eat like we will at the mountain. As always the children are very excited about going. It is hot out there, and most of us wear simple clothes for the trip, sandals and loose-fitting linen wraps.

Only the healthiest animals were suitable for sacrifice.

ANOTHER NARRATOR: So it was. In the years preceding their enslavement, the Hebrew community dwelling in Egypt had for generations made a three-day journey into the desert to Mount Horeb. There they would listen as elders explained the Festival.

READER (at the mountain): These are the laws and customs of our Festival. It is the Festival of Adonay, our God. As we are gathered here together, the children of Israel, descendants of Joseph and his brothers, we thank Adonay for having brought us again to His Mountain, in this season.

Fellow Israelites, let us give thanks.

ALL JOIN IN: The She-hechiyanu.

בָּרוּךְ אַתָּה יְיָ אֱלֹהֵינוּ מֶלֶךְ הָעוֹלָם
שֶׁהֶחֱיָנוּ וְקִיְמָנוּ וְהִגִּיעָנוּ לַזְמַן הַזֶּה

Baruch ata Adonay Eloheynu melech haolam
She-hechi-yanu, v-kee-manu, v-higee-yanu,
la-ziman ha-zeh.

Blessed are You Adonay, our King, for keeping us alive, maintaining our identity, and bringing us to this time.

READER: There is always water brought on our pack animals so that we can wash and keep the sacred place clean from all impurities. The senior males, the first-born, supervise.

After making sure our campsites are clean, an elder approves by taking some green desert plant, we call hyssop, and dipping it in water and sprinkling it around.

5

מַצָּה

Before our enslavement, the Firstborn sons offered unleavened bread to Adonay at Mount Horeb. There were three types: baked with or without oil, and grilled with oil. After enslavement, with pilgrimage forbidden, the holiday moved indoors. Most of the Firstborn had been taken away, and all the People joined in performing their roles, uniting as a nation of Priests.

And the firstborn males in our families take a piece of each kind of matzah—fried in oil, baked, and spread with oil—and hold it up as an offering to Adonay, then toss it on the fire to be fully burnt. It may not sound like a big deal—but offering the three kinds of matzah was something only they could do. It made them especially holy to Adonay—Our firstborn were His Firstborn.

The animals were salted, and then cooked over roasting fires, as was natural in the outdoors. The blood from the sacrificed animals, containing God's power of life—was never eaten, but was sprinkled around the camp-sites to keep away anything that might cause them illness.

NARRATOR: Let us all close our eyes and MEDITATE on that time of blessing before we were made slaves in Egypt.

Now let us say the blessing together, and drink the cup of happiness under the full moon of that Nisan night long ago. We must take within us the strength of that time, for later on we will need all our courage to break free.

ALL JOIN IN BRACHA OVER FIRST CUP OF WINE

בָּרוּךְ אַתָה יְיָ אֱלֹהֵינוּ מֶלֶךְ הָעוֹלָם בּוֹרֵא פְּרִי הַגָּפֶן.

Baruch ata Adonay Eloheynu melech ha-olam
boray piree ha-ga-fayn.

Blessed are you Adonay our King, Creator of
the fruit of the vine.

The Kiddush:

בָּרוּךְ אַתָה יְיָ אֱלֹהֵינוּ מֶלֶךְ הָעוֹלָם אֲשֶׁר בָּחַר בָּנוּ מִכָּל עָם וְרוֹמְמָנוּ
מִכָּל לָשׁוֹן וְקִדְּשָׁנוּ בְּמִצְוֹתָיו . וַתִּתֶּן לָנוּ יְיָ אֱלֹהֵינוּ בְּאַהֲבָה מוֹעֲדִים
לְשִׂמְחָה חַגִּים וּזְמַנִּים לְשָׂשׂוֹן אֶת יוֹם חַג הַמַצוֹת הַזֶה זְמַן חֵרוּתֵנוּ
מִקְרָא קֹדֶשׁ זֵכֶר לִיצִיאַת מִצְרָיִם. כִּי בָנוּ בָחַרְתָ וְאוֹתָנוּ קִדַּשְׁתָ מִכָּל
הָעַמִים וּמוֹעֲדֵי קָדְשֶׁךָ בְּשִׂמְחָה וּבְשָׂשׂוֹן הִנְחַלְתָנוּ. בָּרוּךְ אַתָה יְיָ
מְקַדֵּשׁ יִשְׂרָאֵל וְהַזְמַנִים.

NARRATOR: Much later, after the Exodus, the firstborn would be replaced by the Kohanim—the priests. And they too would offer Adonay the three matzot as part of their consecration ceremony. But back then—before they were made slaves—the People depended on their firstborn sons to join the elders, supervising the sacrifice and ritual requirements.

READER: For more than three centuries, generations of Hebrews had lived in Egypt. Until Seti came to power, we had felt at home. His campaigns in Canaan against Hebrews still living there were victorious—but somehow they were not our victory. Our hearts and loyalty were to his enemy—our fellow Hebrews, and we had begun to feel like outsiders. Even though we lived alongside our Egyptian neighbors, and they too were descendants from Abraham, we felt different. Theirs was a world full of so-called gods while we worshipped the God of our ancestors, Adonay, and no other.

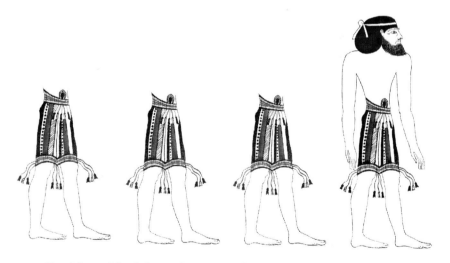

Fashionable fringed garments worn by Hebrew men long before Moses (see the wall painting pictured on page 38), were signs of cultural identity and keeping Adonay's commandments. Today, fringes still adorn the talit, our traditional prayer shawl.

READER: And then Seti died. His son, a thin-faced man with sharp features, became the new Pharoh. He spoke of building great cities and making Egypt the center of the world. He pointed to all the things that had shamed Egypt in the past. Foreigners had always thought they could conquer Egypt, he said. The Hyksos had even succeeded for a time. Now there were the Hebrews. He said, "if they keep increasing in numbers, they may join the Habiru living in Canaan and lay siege to all of Egypt." This Pharoh was named Ramses.

READER: The tenth of Nisan was again approaching and we were all selecting our lambs for the pilgrimage to Horeb. That's when the Pharoh's officers came. They brought laws with them. The Pharoh had ordered that Hebrews have no more male children. If they did have a son, it would be put to death.

READER: Equally devastating, we were told we could not make the pilgrimage to Horeb. Our people would be the Pharoh's workers, slaves to build his new cities. We would be used to make mudbricks for walls. He took thousands of our young men and then thousands more. He pulled us apart from our families and homes.

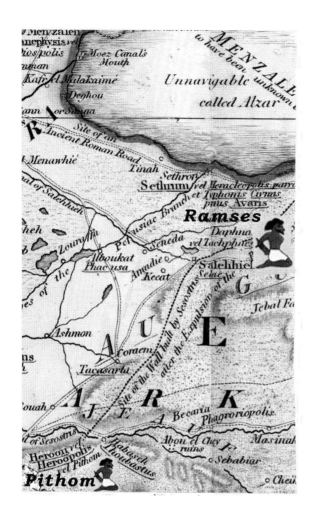

Taking thousands of fit men as slaves, Ramses hoped to achieve two goals: He would build great cities with our forced labor, and destroy our potential military alliance with Hebrews living in Canaan.

NARRATOR: In that time, Hebrew husbands and wives slept apart, terrified of having a baby boy and witnessing its murder. But some couples were already expecting a child, such as Yochaved and Amram from the tribe of Levi.

When their baby was being born, two sympathetic Hebrew midwives, Shifra and Puah, helped deliver the child. To save it, hoping for a miracle, Yochaved and Amram made a small reed basket for it to float on the river. Perhaps a kind Egyptian would rescue their child. No, not all Egyptians were heartless. Many felt sympathy.

One who did was the Pharoh's own daughter. While bathing in the Nile, she noticed the reed basket. When she saw the infant inside, her first words were, "This must be a Hebrew child."

And she rescued the boy, naming him Moses, meaning "he has been drawn from the water."

Her act of kindness knew no limit. She handed the baby to Moses' sister, Miriam, who was watching nearby. Moses would be brought to his own mother, and nursed properly. Yoachaved and Amram had had a miracle from God. The Pharoh's own daughter had saved their son.

The Pharoh's edict ordering the death of newborn Hebrew males caused a rift in some Egyptian circles. Having come to bathe in the Nile, Ramses' own daughter took notice of Moses' floating basket and rescued him. She observed, "This must be a Hebrew child."

ANOTHER NARRATOR: Over the next decades, the lives of our People changed drastically. The Egyptian taskmasters oppressed the Hebrew slaves with hard labor, forcing them to meet a daily quota of bricks. If they grew tired, they were beaten. But the Pharoh was shrewd. Instead of making the slavery so hard they would rebel, he had others pull up the straw stumps from harvested wheat fields, straw to be mixed with the clay to give the bricks strength. And he let the older people, the ones over fifty, and the children stay at home. So Hebrew families didn't just fall apart. At least the Pharoh didn't confiscate their property or possessions. At home, they could still afford good foods like onions, leeks and pomegranites. Also our people had vineyards and herds of animals.

READER: One of the biggest changes was that before too many years passed, the younger generation had no recollection of the pilgrimage to Horeb.

A YOUNG READER: Our parents knew what had been done at Horeb, and every year in the month of Nisan they did the same thing in our houses. First, we cleaned the house from anything leavened. And we roasted a special salted lamb. The salt was a blessing from God because it stopped food from going bad and getting smelly.

Oh yeah—we dipped hyssop into water and sprinkled it all around.

NARRATOR (seder leader, after **washing hands**): Let us recall the blessing of salt and its importance to our ancestors, keeping their food from spoiling, and protecting them from sickness.

And let us DIP parsely into salty water, recalling how they once used hyssop to sprinkle cleansing water—and thank Adonay for the blessing of the new season.

ALL DIP AND RECITE THE BLESSING OVER THE KARPAS

בָּרוּךְ אַתָּה יְיָ אֱלֹהֵינוּ מֶלֶךְ הָעוֹלָם בּוֹרֵא פְּרִי הָאֲדָמָה.

Baruch ata Adonay Elohaynu melech ha-olam bo-ray piree ha-adamah.

Blessed are You Adonay, our King, Creator of the earth's vegetation.

A FIRSTBORN PARTICIPANT HOLDS UP THE THREE-TIERED PLATE OF MATZAH and says:

In the tradition of that time, we offer this bread to Adonay. This was the bread offered by the firstborn, which all the People ate at Horeb when they were free—the pure bread.

While slaves, they all acted like the firstborn, or elders, carrying out the Horeb ceremonies in their own homes, making their houses clean and pure for Adonay, and teaching the meaning of the Festival to their children. In the period of slavery, with so many of the firstborn taken from their homes, everybody held the three kinds up to Adonay—offering Him their complete devotion—and so it was that Adonay accepted their offering and all Hebrews were consecrated as His Firstborn—a nation of priests.

Praying they would again be free, free to worship at Horeb, free even to return to the Land of Canaan, the people held the three kinds of unleavened bread aloft and said something like this:

ALL SAY "Ha lachma Anya" "Let all who are hungry come in and eat!"

הָא לַחְמָא עַנְיָא דִי אֲכַלוּ אַבְהָתָנָא בְּאַרְעָא דְמִצְרָיִם.

Ha-lachma anya dee acha-lu avhatana bi-ar-ah di-meets-ra-yim.

This is the bread eaten in slavery, and eaten by our ancestors in Egypt before they were enslaved.

כָּל דִכְפִין יֵיתֵי וְיֵכֻל כָּל דִצְרִיךְ יֵיתֵי וְיִפְסַח.

Kal deech-feen yaytay v'yay-chul kal deets-reech yaytay v'yeefsach.

Let all who are hungry come eat with us, let all who are needy share our Pesach feast.

הָשַׁתָּא הָכָא לַשָׁנָה הַבָּאָה בְּאַרְעָא דְיִשְׂרָאֵל.

Ha-shata hacha la-shana ha-ba-ah bi-ar-ah di-yees-ra-el.

We are here now--next year in the land of Israel.

הָשַׁתָּא עַבְדֵי לַשָׁנָה הַבָּאָה בְּנֵי חוֹרִין.

Ha-shata avday la-sha-na ha-ba-ah binay chor-een.

Now we are slaves--next year we will be free!

NARRATOR: In our time, it is customary to break in half our middle matzah—and hide it as the AFIKOMEN. How ancient is this practice called YACHATS? Perhaps it was initiated in the time of slavery to express dismay at the sundering of our People in half. (The Afikomen is hidden).

READER: It was not easy to celebrate the holiday with most of our firstborn taken off into forced labor—since they were usually the men over twenty, and most fit.

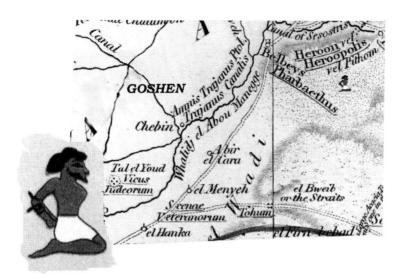

The site of Goshen has been identified from historical sources as well as archeological finds, including unique pottery. Centered at "Tel Yehud" (Tal el Youd, in Latin), the community extended north and east. The city of Pithom was likely situated on its border, facilitating the transportation and exploitation of Hebrew slaves.

ALL READ Avadim Ha-yinu in English translation—then join in singing the Hebrew.

We were slaves to Pharoh in Egypt and Adonay took us out from there with a powerful outstretched arm. And, if the Holy One, blessed is He, had not taken out our ancestors from Egypt, then all our People's children, and their children and children's children would have remained slaves to the Pharohs of Egypt--and we too would still be in Egypt, a People lost to slavery. Therefore, even if all of us are wise, even if we understand the story of Passover, even if we are revered as elders, even if we are scholars of Torah--we are commanded to relate the details of our Exodus from Egypt. And the more one expands on the themes of the Exodus, the more praiseworthy one is.

עֲבָדִים הָיִינוּ לְפַרְעֹה בְּמִצְרַיִם וַיּוֹצִיאֵנוּ יְיָ אֱלֹהֵינוּ מִשָּׁם בְּיָד חֲזָקָה וּבִזְרוֹעַ נְטוּיָה. וְאִלּוּ לֹא הוֹצִיא הַקָּדוֹשׁ בָּרוּךְ הוּא אֶת אֲבוֹתֵינוּ מִמִּצְרַיִם הֲרֵי אָנוּ וּבָנֵינוּ וּבְנֵי בָנֵינוּ מְשֻׁעְבָּדִים הָיִינוּ לְפַרְעֹה בְּמִצְרָיִם. וַאֲפִילוּ כֻּלָּנוּ חֲכָמִים כֻּלָּנוּ נְבוֹנִים כֻּלָּנוּ זְקֵנִים כֻּלָּנוּ יוֹדְעִים אֶת הַתּוֹרָה מִצְוָה עָלֵינוּ לְסַפֵּר בִּיצִיאַת מִצְרָיִם וְכָל הַמַּרְבֶּה לְסַפֵּר בִּיצִיאַת מִצְרַיִם הֲרֵי זֶה מְשֻׁבָּח.

15

Avadeem hayeenu lipharoh bimeetsra-yeem vayotsee-yaynu Adonay
Elohaynu meesham bi-yad chazaka u-veez-roah nitu-ya. Vi-eelu lo
hotsie ha-kadosh baruch hu et avotaynu mee mitsra-yeem haray anu
u-va-naynu u-vinay va-naynu mi-shu-ba-deem ha-yeenu lipharo
bimeets-rayeem. Va-afeelu ku-lanu cha-cha-meem, ku-lanu nivo-
neem, ku-lanu zikay-neem, ku-lanu yo-deem et ha-torah meets-vah
alayneu lisapayr bee-tsee-yat meets-rayeem. vi-chal ha-marbeh
lisa-payr bee-tsee-yat meets-ra-yeem haray zeh mishu-bach.

And we never lost faith. We were determined that when
Adonay freed us, we would make His pilgrimage. That's
why we bought our lambs four days early—usually on
the 10th of Nisan. Afterall, it was a three day walk to the
mountain. We'd have to leave on the 11th, to get there
on time. Like we used to do before there was slavery.

READER: Yes, the night before, we even cleaned out the
house making sure there was no Hamayts. All of us
shared in the household holiday. If there weren't enough
of us because of the slavery we'd get neighbors to join
us. And we did the same things we did at Horeb, pretty
much. We dressed for the lamb dinner wearing sandals
and travelling clothes, and keeping our walking sticks
handy. We wanted Adonay to see we were ready to go to
Horeb.

YOUNG READER: It was weird to see our parents going
around sprinkling everything with water from a branch
they'd dipped into it. And you wouldn't believe they did
it with the lamb's blood too. Mostly around the area of
the fire pit. I think they hoped we'd ask why we were
doing the two dips.

A YOUNG READER ASKS: Why does somebody dip a
branch with green leaves in water and sprinkle it
around?

A READER ANSWERS: Our God is a God of Life, and we show Him we will take care of this precious gift, by making sure nothing unclean makes it dirty. And our Hyssop branch is perfect for sprinkling. It has good branches and leaves, just right to remember the new season.

ANOTHER YOUNG READER: Even if we don't ask, they tell us. The blood part I remember. We sprinkle it around the roasting pit because it is full of Adonay's power of life.

Attested as a post-escape, anti-plague ritual (Levit. 14:51), the Hebrew priests dipped hyssop into the blood of a bird, and applied it to the doorways of their tents and houses. The use of lamb's blood to ward off the tenth plague, is the pre-Exodus enactment of a similar ritual.

A READER: Once everything is washed—including our-selves—we take the flour from our sacks, and make the bread. You may fry it in oil. Or mix it with oil and bake it—or you can simply make wafers from flour which you mix with a little water and eat with oil spread on them. Do not let the damp flour sit for more than a few moments before you heat it—otherwise it will not remain pure.

ANOTHER YOUNG READER: The unleavened bread isn't bad. I like the matzah mixed with olive oil—but still it is odd not to have regular pita. And yes, I always ask why we are only eating these three kinds of matzah. Of course, I can't remember the answer.

ANOTHER YOUNG READER ASKS: Why is this bread different from all other bread—when all other bread can be eaten after it rises, but not this bread?

A READER ANSWERS: All other bread is touched by the same thing that changes damp walls from white to green, and gives off the smell of something unclean. You have seen old bread turn green. People too can be touched by it—and their skin may become reddish, and scaly. The pure bread is the only bread we offer to Adonay.

ADULT READER: If we don't tell them, who will? On this night of our Festival—though we are slaves—and many of our firstborn have been taken off to do forced labor, we are a Nation of Firstborn—Adonay's priests. Just as it was at Horeb, it is still. Therefore we offer and eat the sacred bread consecrating us to God as His priests. If the Pharoh thinks he has ruined us by taking our first-born as slaves, he is wrong. We Hebrews are all Adonay's firstborn.

NARRATOR: And—it was a custom ever since Horeb to eat only unleavened bread for seven days—because it took three days to get to Horeb and three days to get back—and they couldn't mix leavened bread with unleavened bread while they were travelling. In our own time, we too have questions—four of them, somewhat changed by time and memory.

Young participants lead in singing

THE FOUR QUESTIONS

מַה נִשְׁתַּנָה הַלַּיְלָה הַזֶּה מִכָּל הַלֵּילוֹת?

שֶׁבְּכָל הַלֵּילוֹת אָנוּ אוֹכְלִין חָמֵץ וּמַצָּה הַלַּיְלָה הַזֶּה כֻּלוֹ מַצָּה.

שֶׁבְּכָל הַלֵּילוֹת אָנוּ אוֹכְלִין שְׁאָר יְרָקוֹת הַלַּיְלָה הַזֶּה מָרוֹר.

שֶׁבְּכָל הַלֵּילוֹת אֵין אָנוּ מַטְבִּילִין אֲפִילוּ פַּעַם אֶחָת הַלַּיְלָה הַזֶּה שְׁתֵּי פְעָמִים.

שֶׁבְּכָל הַלֵּילוֹת אָנוּ אוֹכְלִין בֵּין יוֹשְׁבִין וּבֵין מְסֻבִּין הַלַּיְלָה הַזֶּה כֻּלָּנוּ מְסֻבִּין.

Ma nishtana ha lye-lah ha-zeh mee-kal ha-laylot?

She-bi-chal ha-lay-lot anu och-lin cha-maytz u-matzah ha-lye-la hazeh kulo matzah?

She-bi-chal ha-lay-lot anu och-lin shi-ar yi-ra-kot ha-lye-lah hazeh maror?

She-bi-chal ha-lay-lot ayn anu matbeeleen a-fee-lu pa-am e-chat ha-lye-lah hazeh sh'tay fi-a-meem?

She-bi-chal ha-lay-lot anu och-lin bayn yosh-veen u-vayn mi-su-been ha-lye-lah hazeh ku-lanu mi-su-been?

Why is this night different from all other nights:

...when on other nights we eat leavened grain, as well as matzah-- but tonight we only eat matzah?

19

...when on all other nights we eat any kind of vegetables we want--
but tonight we have to eat bitter ones too?

...when on all other nights we don't dip anything into anything even
once--but tonight we dip twice?

...when on all other nights we sit either upright or leaning--but
tonight everybody reclines?

ANOTHER NARRATOR: But despite questions and doubts,
they put on a cheerful face. Yet in their hearts the enslaved
Hebrews were torn between faith and dispair. Nobody
could speak for them. The one who had seemed a leader
was Moses. But he had fled, some said because he'd killed
a vicious Egyptian taskmaster—others suspected he was
forced into exile because of his outspoken defense of his
People's rights.

Then the news came. Ramses II was dead. Word spread
across the boundaries of nations. And word reached Moses.
Not that he would have thought it safe to return. But
Adonay revealed His will that he do so. Whatever the
new Pharoh's policy toward the Hebrews, he would at
least listen to Moses without arresting him.

Ramses II was dead. Moses, who had been living in exile, was commanded by Adonay at the Burning Bush to tell the new Pharoh, "Let my People go three days into the wilderness" to again celebrate the annual Festival, sacrificing lambs and offering Unleavened Bread. (Exodus 3:18; 5:1)

YOUNG READER: I know I couldn't even pronounce the name of the new guy. Meren-petoo-ie. We'd kind of spit it out.

READER: Speaking as a firstborn son, a slave, I can tell you that when we heard Moses was back, and that he and Aaron had gone to Merenptah–who was Ramses' son—demanding our right to go to Horeb, we were ecstatic. But the Pharoh not only refused, he made us work even harder. Now we had to gather the straw to mix with the clay for bricks. It's not easy pulling up stubborn clumps of straw—and our daily quota of bricks was the same!

READER (a slave): It's murder under the hot sun. People just moan and groan and cry. Nobody believes Moses when he says Adonay is telling him what to say and do.

NARRATOR: And then the miracles started.

YOUNG READER: The water has turned red like blood. It's slimey. Like stuff is growing all in it. Red gook.

NARRATOR: Blood-red algae had bloomed on the Nile, and appeared in all the streams of Egypt. Ordinary people who had nothing against the Hebrews were desperate for something to drink. Their suffering should bring us no joy—

THEREFORE—let us say the name of this plague on Egypt, and remove from our glasses of wine and grape-juice, a drop to symbolize the fact we take no pleasure in their misery.

ALL SAY "DAM"— דַם "Bloody algae in the water" and dip a finger in our cups removing a drop.

READER: If the Pharoh thought Adonay has no power, he was re-thinking that notion. So, when the fish in the river died, and the frogs came up out of the water—he seemed ready to make a deal. At least that was the rumor.

Word had it, just a donkey-day south, the Nile water had begun to smell so bad you couldn't go near it without wrapping a piece of cloth around your face. That's what a lot of the Egyptians were doing...digging for clear water along the river bank. But it was all bad.

YOUNG READER: When the crabs and clams and eels got sick, the Egyptian kids started catching them for food. My brother told me that the fish that live near the bottom were eating all the dead fish too. If we eat the bottom fish we'll get sick too. You can tell which ones they are because they don't have any fins or scales like normal fish.

NARRATOR: As the red algae continued to suck the oxygen out of the water, and the air-starved frogs emerged to breath in the baking sun, they needed shade to survive—shade of houses, so they found their way into food pantries, and even the bedding of the Egyptians. Most Hebrews lived away from the river, and were spared the frogs. Instead of water, they drank the juice of the fruits—especially grapes from the vines they had planted over the years.

Meanwhile, the frogs were all dying, and zillions of them were heaped in huge mounds along the river bank.

ALL SAY: "TSIFARDAYAH" צְפַרְדֵּעַ "Frogs" and dip a drop of wine from the cup.

Moses had warned the Pharoh—but he still didn't get the message. The putrifying frogs attracted insect swarms.

ALL SAY: "KINNIM" כִּנִּים "insects"—removing another drop of wine.

The kinnim were eating the putrid frogs and became carriers of contagion. When they came in contact with the cattle they made them sick.

Jackals, hyenas, foxes and desert tigers were coming close to the towns looking for water. It wasn't just that they were dangerous. But they had begun to hunt among the domestic herds.

WILD BEASTS

עָרוֹב

As starving wilderness wildlife migrated toward the populated Nile Basin, people were attacked and carcasses of uncommon prey lay about, ravaged and torn.

ALL SAY: "AROV" עָרוֹב "wild beasts" and dip a drop of wine from the cup.

The insect swarms sickened the cattle. They developed skin infections and became too weak to stand. Also there was no water for them.

ALL SAY "DEVER" דֶבֶר "cattle disease" and dip a drop from the cup.

Other animals like sheep, goats and lambs were also weak and sick—and they'd be torn apart for food by the wild scavanger beasts.

That's when people started getting sick. The Egyptians got boils and skin diseases. The insects were causing serious illness to people, not just animals.

24

ALL SAY "SHECHIN" שְׁחִין "boils" and dip a drop from the cup.

צְפַרְדֵעַ

כִּנִּים

שְׁחִין

Kinnim (insects) feeding on Tsifardayah (dead frogs) infected people, causing Shecheen (boils).

READER: When the Pharoh realized only the Egyptians were getting sick, he wanted a meeting with Moses.

And Moses told the Pharoh the plagues were a punishment by Adonay—and would only be stopped if he'd let the People be free from slavery, and worship at Horeb as was our custom before slavery.

YOUNG READER: Meanwhile, our parents have been very strict about what we should and shouldn't do. Under no circumstances are we allowed to eat anything without washing first—and they don't want us even touching our animals. Since the insects like to land on the sheep and goats, we've been told not to get near them. Only the older people who can tell if an animal is sick are allowed to do the milking.

ANOTHER YOUNG READER: Of course the wild animals don't care. They'll spot a sick cow or lamb and attack it. Almost everyday we find a goat that's been killed and torn apart. So our parents have warned us, animals that have died because they are sick, or were killed and torn apart are not food. If we touch or eat them we can get very sick.

ANOTHER YOUNG READER: The elders are still around to examine the animals just as our older, firstborn brothers, had always done—that is before they were taken away as slaves. You could only sacrifice a perfect animal to Adonay. That's how come they knew an animal was sick—everybody always pays attention in case it is no good for our offerings.

NARRATOR: For awhile there was enough healthy food. The fruits and greens were abundant as springtime arrived. The barley crop was filling out the fields. And the boils were not fatal. The Egyptians who were eating the meat of sick cattle were too few in number for anybody to notice. The rich Egyptians, such as the Pharoh's household, were able to be selective when choosing a prime rib for supper.

READER: In the old days, we purchased our sacrificial lambs four days before the Festival because it was a three-day walk to the mountain. When the plagues struck, those four days were a period of watching the animal closely to make sure it wasn't sick. Of course, the average Egyptian is no good at telling a sick animal from a healthy one. There's even a joke about it. If they can't tell the difference between a god and an animal—how are they going to know which ones to eat?

Now there have been three more plagues to our south. Huge hail has fallen, killing the fruit, and the days have been dark as night. And, we've heard about immense clouds of locusts descending on the barley in the fields.

27

חֹשֶׁךְ   דָּם

**Blood-red algae thickened the Nile with slime.
Later, darkness spread across the land.**

NARRATOR: When the darkness of hailstorm and scourge of locusts lifted, Egypt was faced with famine.

28

ALL SAY:

"BARAD" בָּרָד "hail" and dip a drop of wine from the cup.

"ARBEH" אַרְבֶּה "locusts" and dip a drop.

"CHOSHECH" חשֶׁךְ "darkness" and dip a drop.

Our People didn't really sense the threat. Most of their animals were still ok.

But, in fact, the plagues were extremely dangerous. When Moses and the elders met, they realized Adonay was about to devastate Egypt in a way far more terrifying than had already happened. Death was in the air—not just the death of animals, but of people.

READER: So, we have a few extra locusts, that's what I thought. Until this message arrived—a whispered secret from Moses that he had been instructed by Adonay directly to get the People ready. A plague of death would soon begin.

NARRATOR: Days before the fourteenth of Nisan, the Pharoh became terrified. He saw how sick his people were becoming. The young ones were losing strength to the diseases. One of his own sons seemed a little yellow around the ears.

And summoning his advisors, he asked what he should do about Moses and the Hebrews. They answered him in desperation, saying:

עַד מָתַי יִהְיֶה זֶה לָנוּ לְמוֹקֵשׁ. שַׁלַּח אֶת הָאֲנָשִׁים וְיַעַבְדוּ
אֶת יְהֹוָה אֱלֹהֵיהֶם הֲטֶרֶם תֵּדַע כִּי אָבְדָה מִצְרָיִם.

How long will this man bring us disaster?
Send away that People and let them worship Adonay their God.
Don't you yet see that Egypt is lost?

Ramses II ruled for 67 years from about 1280 B.C.E. He sought the arrest of Moses who had defended his fel-low-Hebrews, killing one of the cruel taskmasters. Scientific analysis of his mummy indicates Ramses may have died of insect-transmitted disease, suggesting the Ten Plagues may have begun toward the end of his life.

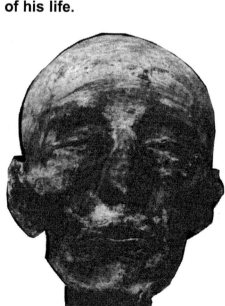

After Ramses' death, Merenptah, his son, became Pharoh and met with Moses. He scoffed at the demand that the Hebrew People be free to celebrate the Festival of Adonay at Mount Horeb.

READER: At last the Pharoh summoned Moses and told him to take all the people—even the slaves and the herds of animals and leave. We couldn't believe it.

Everybody knew this wasn't going to be a trip only to Horeb. Once we were out, we weren't coming back. It was as if Adonay spoke directly to us. We were to take the blood of the slaughtered lamb—and instead of sprinkling it around the roasting pit—put it on the doorposts and lintels of our houses. The coming plague against the Egyptians was going to be so deadly we too were in danger. Only the blood on the doorway having Adonay's power of life would save us.

After the Pharoh let the Hebrew slaves return home from Pithom and Ramses, the herds were gathered and preparations for the Exodus began.

READER (A MOTHER): Sure we have faith—but we've been sprinkling lots of extra water on ourselves, and especially the children, because we are afraid of the plague. Ok, we are roasting our lambs as usual and making kiddush over the wine—but this night is truly different. At midnight, we're leaving.

NARRATOR: Let us close our eyes and MEDITATE on God's promise to protect our People.

BRACHA OVER THE SECOND CUP OF WINE—the cup of faith in our being free to BE. Let us all have the courage to make our personal journeys, though the way be difficult.

בָּרוּךְ אַתָּה יְיָ אֱלֹהֵינוּ מֶלֶךְ הָעוֹלָם בּוֹרֵא פְּרִי הַגָּפֶן.

Baruch ata Adonay Eloheynu melech ha-olam
 boray piree ha-ga-fayn.

Blessed are you Adonay our King, Creator of the fruit of the vine.

32

to making an annual pilgrimage to Mount Horeb, for the Festival of Adonay.
where the pursuing Egyptian army met disaster in the marshy water.
ascended its heights to receive the Ten Commandments.

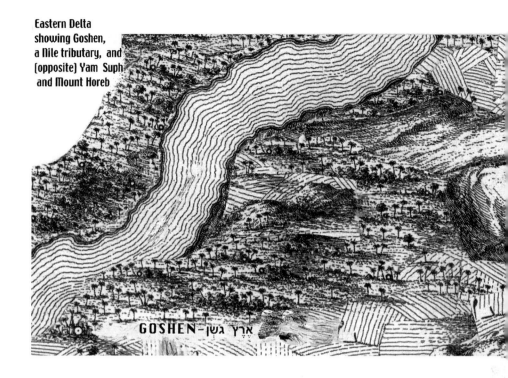

Eastern Delta showing Goshen, a Nile tributary, and (opposite) Yam Suph and Mount Horeb

GOSHEN-אֶרֶץ גֹּשֶׁן

From our homes in Goshen, long before enslavement, we were accustomed
The night of the escape, our people travelled eastward, crossing Yam Suph,
Finally free, we encamped at the foot of Horeb, a million strong and Moses

34

PART TWO

NARRATOR: All of us now wash our hands and recite the blessing.

BRACHA OVER WASHING THE HANDS

בָּרוּךְ אַתָּה יְיָ אֱלֹהֵינוּ מֶלֶךְ הָעוֹלָם אֲשֶׁר קִדְּשָׁנוּ בְּמִצְוֹתָיו
וְצִוָּנוּ עַל נְטִילַת יָדָיִם.

Baruch ata Adonay Elohaynu melech ha-olam asher keed-shanu bi-
mitsvotav vitsee-vanu al niteelat ya-dye-im.

Blessed are You, Adonay our God, who rules the world, making us holy
with His commandments, commanding us to wash our hands.

READER: As a firstborn son, one of thousands back home following the Pharoh's decision to let the Hebrews go, I thank Adonay, and offer the unleavened bread, holding it up—and we all eat the three kinds, consecrating ourselves as Adonay's Firstborn—a Nation of Priests.

BLESSING OVER BREAD AND MATZAH

בָּרוּךְ אַתָּה יְיָ אֱלֹהֵינוּ מֶלֶךְ הָעוֹלָם הַמּוֹצִיא לֶחֶם מִן הָאָרֶץ.

Baruch ata Adonay Elohaynu melech ha-olam ha-motzie lechem min-
ha-arets.

Blessed are You Adonay our God, who rules the world and brings forth
grain from the earth.

בָּרוּךְ אַתָּה יְיָ אֱלֹהֵינוּ מֶלֶךְ הָעוֹלָם אֲשֶׁר קִדְּשָׁנוּ בְּמִצְוֹתָיו
וְצִוָּנוּ עַל אֲכִילַת מַצָּה.

Baruch ata Adonay Elohaynu melech ha-olam asher keed-shanu
bi-mitsvotav vitsee-vanu al acheelat matzah.

Blessed are You Adonay our God, who rules the world, making us holy
with His commandments, commanding us to eat matzah.

35

FEMALE READER (A Mom): Today I scrubbed the house extra clean. Believe me, we're all nervous about leaving. Nothing remains that can become mouldy. Our flour is dry as dust. For days, whatever we've been eating, fruit or cheese, or locusts—they're not as bad as you think, just a little crunchy—have been followed by bitter herbs. Ever since the plagues started, the elders have advised us that this is the best medicine against the plague. It may make your eyes tear and your nose run, but some of our radishes are bitter enough to stop anything bad from turning our insides rotten.

A MOTHER: It's not so simple to get them to eat an extra portion of bitter herbs. But we did.

YOUNG READER: Our moms are amazing. They've made up for our problems with food by inventing delicious recipes. They take dates from our palm trees and figs and moosh them together with citrus stuff like lemons. Oh, and we had nuts mixed in. We don't mind the bitter herbs nearly as much when we dip them in the sweet stuff. They call it Charoset, I think.

NARRATOR: Let us all say the blessing over the bitter herb, and dip it into the Charoset.

BRACHA OVER THE MAROR

בָּרוּךְ אַתָּה יְיָ אֱלֹהֵינוּ מֶלֶךְ הָעוֹלָם אֲשֶׁר קִדְּשָׁנוּ בְּמִצְוֹתָיו וְצִוָּנוּ עַל אֲכִילַת מָרוֹר.

Baruch ata Adonay Elohaynu melech ha-olam asher keed-shanu bi-mitsvotav vitsee-vanu al acheelat maror.

Blessed are You Adonay our God, who rules the world, making us holy with His commandments, commanding us to eat bitter herbs.

36

NEXT, make a sandwich of matzah and bitter herbs—something our sage Hillel taught us, though our ancestors in Egypt had no such pleasure.

We call it KORECH and say the following:

כֵּן עָשָׂה הִלֵּל בִּזְמַן שֶׁבֵּית הַמִּקְדָּשׁ הָיָה קַיָּם.
הָיָה כּוֹרֵךְ מַצָּה וּמָרוֹר וְאוֹכֵל בְּיַחַד
לְקַיֵּם מַה שֶּׁנֶּאֱמַר--עַל מַצּוֹת וּמְרֹרִים יֹאכְלֻהוּ.

**Kayn asa hilayl beezman shebayt ha-mikdash haya ka-yam.
Haya koraych matzah u-maror vi-ochel biyachad lika-yam mah
she-ne-e-mar--al matzot u-mi-ro-reem yoch-lu-hu.**

**This is what Hillel used to do in the days of our ancient Temple.
He combined matzah and bitter herbs and ate them together in order
to perform the Torah command (Exodus 12:8) according to its exact
wording--"matzah and bitter herbs shall you eat."**

READER: As midnight came closer, I can tell you we were scared. Some of our boys were even asking why we had to leave. They hadn't experienced slavery, just the good life. So we explained: We are going out of Egypt because Adonay is leading us to freedom. Our smart sons and daughters understood the value of being free. But the stubborn ones were afraid they'd miss the food once the provisions were gone. Keep talking like that, we warned, and Adonay might leave them behind.

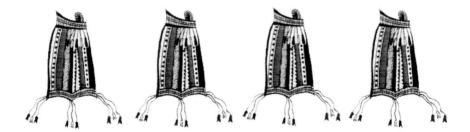

Our uniform style of dress could not conceal differences in attitude and intellectual acumen as plans for the Exodus aroused debate within Hebrew families.

NARRATOR: Some things never change. Kids today don't always realize they are here, free to be Jews, because of the miracles in that time. Instead of saying "WE" they say "YOU"—as if it's all a made up story that has nothing to do with them. So the Torah instructs us teach our children the history. Tell them what happened! The wise one will understand, the wicked one will never care, and the ones who are immature, or too young to understand will simply listen.

Here are passages from the Torah (and one from Ezekiel) along with occasional ancient rabbinic commentary that describe the miracle of Pesach. We read them in turn:

" 'Numbering very few,' as it is said. 'Your forefathers went to Egypt with only seventy people. And now Adonay has multiplied your number like the stars in the heavens.'" (Deut. 10:22)

"'And there the nation was formed.' This teaches us that the People, Israel, became significant there. 'Powerful and strong,' as it is said. 'And the Israelites multiplied and expanded, and were extremely independent. And the land was filled with them.'" (Exodus 1:7)

"'And populous,' as it is said. 'And I caused you to mature into a fertile People, whose grain and produce were beautiful; your budding fields like youthful breasts, your grain like flowing hair—yet, you remained exposed.'" (Ezekiel 16:7)

"And the Pharoh said, 'come let us outwit them, otherwise they will continue to multiply, and may join our enemies and fight us.'" (Exodus 1:10)

"So the Egyptians set taskmasters over us, in order to oppress us with heavy burdens. And we built the store-cities of Pithom and Ramses." (Exodus 1:11)

The Pharoh's new palace was located in Avaris. Renamed "Ramses," and made the capital, the city was built mostly by Hebrew slaves. Impervious to the onset of the plagues, lavish inaugural festivities celebrated its completion.

"'And they imposed hard labor upon us.' As it is written: 'Egypt callously made the Hebrews into slaves.'" (Exodus 1:13)

"And we cried out to Adonay our God, and Adonay heard our voice and saw our misery, our lost hope, and our oppression." (Deut. 26:7)

"'And He saw our misery.' This refers to the misery of having no sex-life for fear of having a son who would be put to death." (Exodus 2:25)

"'And He saw our lost hope.' This refers to the hopelessness that all Hebrews felt when their male babies were drowned by the Pharoh's police. (Exodus 1:22)

"And Adonay said: 'I will pass through the land of Egypt on this night. I and not an angel. I will smite all the newborn in the land of Egypt. I and not a seraph. And to the so-called gods of Egypt I will bring an end. I, and not an emissary. I am Adonay. I am the only God—and there is no other.'" (Exodus 12:12)

"And Adonay brought us out of Egypt with a powerful hand and outstretched arm, with awesome signs and wonders." (Deut. 26:8)

These next two passages link us to earlier generations, thanking God for enabling us to survive. Let us join in singing the first:

Vi-hee-she-amdah la-ah-vo-taynu.

וְהִיא שֶׁעָמְדָה לַאֲבוֹתֵינוּ וְלָנוּ. שֶׁלֹּא אֶחָד בִּלְבָד עָמַד עָלֵינוּ לְכַלּוֹתֵינוּ
אֶלָּא שֶׁבְּכָל דּוֹר וָדוֹר עוֹמְדִים עָלֵינוּ לְכַלּוֹתֵנוּ וְהַקָּדוֹשׁ בָּרוּךְ הוּא מַצִּילֵנוּ
מִיָּדָם.

Vi-hee she am-dah la-avo-taynu vi-lanu. she-lo echad beel-vad
amad aw-laynu li-chalo-taynu aylah she-bi-chal dor vi-dor om-deem
a-laynu li-chalo-taynu vi-ha-kadosh baruch hu mats-ee-laynu mee-
yadam.

This has happened to our ancestors and us--that not just once did
they try and destroy us--but in every generation they have risen
against us to destroy us, and the Holy One, Blessed is He, saves us
from their hand.

בְּכָל דּוֹר וָדוֹר חַיָּב אָדָם לִרְאוֹת אֶת עַצְמוֹ כְּאִלּוּ הוּא יָצָא מִמִּצְרַיִם
שֶׁנֶּאֱמַר וְהִגַּדְתָּ לְבִנְךָ בַּיּוֹם הַהוּא לֵאמֹר בַּעֲבוּר זֶה עָשָׂה יְיָ לִי בְּצֵאתִי
מִמִּצְרָיִם. לֹא אֶת אֲבוֹתֵינוּ בִּלְבָד גָּאַל הַקָּדוֹשׁ בָּרוּךְ הוּא אֶלָּא אַף אוֹתָנוּ
גָּאַל עִמָּהֶם שֶׁנֶּאֱמַר--וְאוֹתָנוּ הוֹצִיא מִשָּׁם לְמַעַן הָבִיא אֹתָנוּ לָתֶת לָנוּ
אֶת הָאָרֶץ אֲשֶׁר נִשְׁבַּע לַאֲבֹתֵינוּ.

Bi-chal dor va-dor cha-yav adam leer-ot et ats-mo ki-eelu hu ya-tsa
mee-meets-ra-yeem she-ne-emar vi-hee-ga-data li-veencha ba-yom
ha-hu lai-mor ba-avur zeh asa Adonay lee bi-tsay-tee mee-meets-
ra-yeem. lo et avo-taynu beelvad ga-al ha-ka-dosh ba-ruch hu, ay-
leh af otanu ga-al eema-hem --vi-otanu ho-tsie mee-sham li-ma-an
havee otanu latet lanu et ha-arets asher neesh-ba la-avo-taynu.

In every generation it is an obligation for each person to view himself
as if he personally escaped from Egypt. As it is said in the Torah, "You
shall tell your offspring on the Festival of Passover, this ceremony is
because Adonay took me out of Egypt." (Exodus 13:8) Not only our
ancestors were saved, by the Holy One, blessed is He, but we too
were saved with them--as it says in the Torah: "We were taken out in
order to bring us to our land, and to give the land to us--as promised
our ancestors."
(Deut. 6:23)

Then, as the full moon was rising that fateful night, it
was time to EAT THE MEAL.

BITAY-AH-VONE! (Good appetite!) We all EAT.

TOWARDS the end of the MEAL:

NARRATOR: It was a moment we never want to forget! How do we remember it? We drink THE THIRD CUP OF WINE—a toast to Adonay's promise—that He will protect us on our way to our own land of Milk and Honey—in our lives now, as in the time of our escape from bondage.

בָּרוּךְ אַתָּה יְיָ אֱלֹהֵינוּ מֶלֶךְ הָעוֹלָם בּוֹרֵא פְּרִי הַגָּפֶן.

Baruch ata Adonay Eloheynu melech ha-olam
boray piree ha-ga-fayn.

Blessed are you Adonay our King, Creator of
the fruit of the vine.

And now we invite the prophet Elijah (who lived nearly five hundred years after the Exodus) to join us! If any of us feel enslaved by difficult circumstances, Elijah will come and share our prayers for freedom. If we don't feel worthy, Elijah brings reassurance. Even our ancestors made a golden calf once in awhile.

THE DOOR IS OPENED. ALL SING Eliyahu HaNavi

אֵלִיָּהוּ הַנָּבִיא אֵלִיָּהוּ הַתִּשְׁבִּי אֵלִיָּהוּ אֵלִיָּהוּ אֵלִיָּהוּ הַגִּלְעָדִי
בִּמְהֵרָה יָבֹא אֵלֵינוּ עִם מָשִׁיחַ בֶּן דָּוִד.

ELEE-YAHU HA-NAVI ELEE-YAHU HA-TISH-BEE ELEE YAHU ELEE YA-HU ELEE
YAHU HA-GEEL-A-DEE BEEM HAY-RA YA-VO AY-LAYNU EEM MA-SHEEACH
BEN DA-VEED...(repeats).

Elijah the prophet, Elijah from Tishbi, Elijah from Gil-ad, may he come speedily to us ushering in the messianic time, recalling that of King David.

Next, we all taste a special last bite of matzah—the dessert matzah. Who has the AFIKOMEN?

NARRATOR (continuing after the Afikomen is eaten): Now let us join in BIRKAT HA-MAZON (thanking Adonay for our food).

רַבּוֹתַי נְבָרֵךְ

Rabo-tye ni-var-aych
Friends, let us make a blessing.

יְהִי שֵׁם יְיָ מְבֹרָךְ מֵעַתָּה וְעַד עוֹלָם
Yi-hee shaym Adonay mivo-rach may-ata vi-ad o-lam.
Let the name of Adonay be praised, now and forever.

בִּרְשׁוּת רַבּוֹתַי נְבָרֵךְ אֱלֹהֵינוּ שֶׁאָכַלְנוּ מִשֶּׁלּוֹ
Beer-shute rabo-tye niva-raych Elohaynu she-achalnu mee-she-lo.
May we all thank Adonay, provider of the food we have just eaten.

בָּרוּךְ אֱלֹהֵינוּ שֶׁאָכַלְנוּ מִשֶּׁלּוֹ וּבְטוּבוֹ חָיִינוּ
Baruch Elohaynu she-achalnu mee-she-lo u-vi-tuvo cha-yeenu.
Blessed is our God whose food we have eaten and whose goodness keeps us alive.

בָּרוּךְ אַתָּה יְיָ אֱלֹהֵינוּ מֶלֶךְ הָעוֹלָם הַזָּן אֶת הָעוֹלָם כֻּלּוֹ בְּטוּבוֹ
בְּחֵן בְּחֶסֶד וּבְרַחֲמִים הוּא נוֹתֵן לֶחֶם לְכָל בָּשָׂר כִּי לְעוֹלָם חַסְדּוֹ
וּבְטוּבוֹ הַגָּדוֹל תָּמִיד לֹא חָסַר לָנוּ וְאַל יֶחְסַר לָנוּ מָזוֹן לְעוֹלָם וָעֶד.
בַּעֲבוּר שְׁמוֹ הַגָּדוֹל כִּי הוּא זָן וּמְפַרְנֵס לַכֹּל וּמֵטִיב לַכֹּל וּמֵכִין מָזוֹן
לְכָל בְּרִיּוֹתָיו אֲשֶׁר בָּרָא. בָּרוּךְ אַתָּה יְיָ הַזָּן אֶת הַכֹּל.

Baruch ata Adonay Elohaynu melech ha-olam hazan et ha-olam kulo
bitu-vo bi-chayn bi-chesed u-vi-ra-cha-meem hu notayn lechem
li-chal basar kee li-olam chas-do u-vi-tuvo ha-gadol ta-meed lo
chasar la-nu vi-al yech-sar lanu mazon li-olam va-ed. Ba-avoor
shemo ha-gadol kee hu zan u-mi-farness la-kol u-mayteev la-kol
u-may-cheen mazon li-chal biree-yo-tav asher bara. Baruch ata
Adonay hazan et ha-kol.

Blessed are You Adonay, who rules the world, giving sustenance and
food to all living things with unlimited compassion, enabling all your
creation to find provision, by joining together to harvest the riches
of the earth.

Next we sing a selection from Hallel, thanking Adonay for the continuing miracles that shape our lives. (ALL SING: Yivarech—Psalm 115)

יְיָ זְכָרָנוּ יְבָרֵךְ
יְבָרֵךְ אֶת בֵּית יִשְׂרָאֵל יְבָרֵךְ אֶת בֵּית אַהֲרֹן
יְבָרֵךְ יִרְאֵי יְיָ הַקְּטַנִּים עִם הַגְּדֹלִים
יֹסֵף יְיָ עֲלֵיכֶם עֲלֵיכֶם וְעַל בְּנֵיכֶם בְּרוּכִים אַתֶּם לַיְיָ
עֹשֵׂה שָׁמַיִם וָאָרֶץ.
הַשָּׁמַיִם שָׁמַיִם לַיְיָ וְהָאָרֶץ נָתַן לִבְנֵי אָדָם
לֹא הַמֵּתִים יְהַלְלוּ יָהּ וְלֹא כָּל יֹרְדֵי דוּמָה
וַאֲנַחְנוּ נְבָרֵךְ יָהּ מֵעַתָּה וְעַד עוֹלָם
הַלְלוּיָהּ.

Adonay zicharanu yiva-raych
yiva-raych et bayt yisrael yiva-raych et bayt aharon
yiva-raych yeer-aye Adonay ha-kitan-eem eem ha-gidol-eem
yosayf Adonay alay-chem alay-chem vi-al binay-chem
biru-cheem atem La-donay oseh sha-mye-eem va-arets.
ha-sha-mye-eem Ladonay vi-ha-arets natan leev-nay adam
lo ha-may-teem yiha-lilu-yah vi-lo kal yorday dumah
va-anach-nu ni-va-raych Yah may-ata vi-ad olam
Halilu-yah.

Adonay remembers us with blessings
He will bless the House of Israel, He will bless the House of Aaron
He will bless those who revere Him--small and great alike.
He will add to your numbers, and to your children's numbers.
Blessed are you by Adonay, Creator of the heavens and the earth.
The heavens belong to Adonay, the earth He has given to mankind.
It is for us the living to praise Adonay forever, and not contemplate
blessings in the hereafter. Ha-li-lu-yah!

READER: It felt like midnight by the time we were done—and we were just getting started. All helped with cleaning up—so there'd be no leftovers to become putrid. The men gathered our herds of sheep and goats. There'd be plenty of food for about three months.

Four days before our escape, the herds were gathered and examined and the sacrificial animals were chosen.

Many of our Egyptian neighbors were happy for us—and gave us farewell gifts. Everything seemed to be changing for the better. Egyptians too would be spared the final plague—we hoped. This time the Pharoh wouldn't go back on his word.

READER: Whether Merenptah changed his mind or plotted to massacre all of us once we left the populated delta region, I don't know. But he ordered his forces to assemble and prepare for pursuit.

And Adonay saw his intention and the plague—the 10th—struck down those who were weakest all across Egypt. Those who were first to be born as the plague struck, newborn babies, too weak to survive—animals as well as people—were all dying. Even the Pharoh lost a son. It was as if Adonay wanted the Egyptians to see they were being punished for making His Firstborn nation slaves.

NARRATOR: Therefore, let us dip a last drop from our wine cups, not to rejoice over MAKAT BICHOROT

ALL SAY: "MAKAT BICHOROT" מַכַּת בְּכֹרוֹת "Death of those first to be born during the plague."

NARRATOR: At Midnight—the fifteenth of Nisan—our People began their hurried departure from Egypt. And the only bread they took with them was unleavened bread since it was their custom to eat it for seven days—the travelling time to Horeb and back.

READER: Well, you who recall us tonight know that not just we—but you—were saved by Adonay. I can only say it was more than we expected, to have reached the shore of that lake called Yam Suph, crossing it without drowning. Not so blessed were Pharoh's army who got caught in the surging waters and many of them drowned.

Yam Suph always had tricky tides.

I hope you who recall us will not forget all the miracles that followed. We were given the Ten Commandments at

46

Horeb soon after, followed by the Torah, and the Shabbat as a sign of Adonay's eternal promise—that we would always have Israel as our land, and one day live there as a People in peace.

NARRATOR: It should have been enough if we only had a few such miracles—but so many! DA-YENU!

By now, we have had too much wine to know the difference between enough and not enough.

So, we read these passages, giving thanks that Adonay did more for us than we ever might have imagined.

In turn:

If Adonay had divided Yam Suph for us--but not drowned our pursuers in it--Dayenu--it would have been good enough for us!

If Adonay had drowned our pursuers in the sea, but not brought us to Mount Horeb--Dayenu---it would have been good enough for us!

If Adonay had given us the Shabbat, but not given us His Commandments at the Mountain--Dayenu--it would have been good enough for us!

If Adonay had brought us to Mount Horeb, but not taken care of us crossing the desert--Dayenu--it would have been good enough for us!

If Adonay protected us from enemies in the desert, but had not fed us manna--Dayenu--it would have been good enough for us!

If Adonay had fed us manna, and not brought us into the Land of Israel--Dayenu--it would have been good enough for us!

AND, ALL JOIN IN:

EELU HOTZIE HOTZIE-YANU

HOTZIYANU MEE-MITSRAYIM

DAYAYNU (Da Da Yaynu, Da Da Yaynu,

Dayaynu, Da-yaynu!)

EELU NATAN NATAN LANU

NATAN LANU ET HA-SHABBAT

DAYAYNU ...

EELU NATAN NATAN LANU

NATAN LANU ET HA-TORAH

DAYAYNU...

אֵלּוּ הוֹצִיא הוֹצִיאָנוּ
הוֹצִיאָנוּ מִמִּצְרַיִם דַּיֵּנוּ

אֵלּוּ נָתַן נָתַן לָנוּ
נָתַן לָנוּ אֶת הַשַּׁבָּת דַּיֵּנוּ

אֵלּוּ נָתַן נָתַן לָנוּ
נָתַן לָנוּ אֶת הַתוֹרָה דַּיֵּנוּ

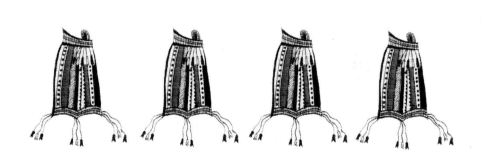

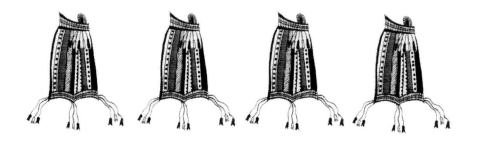

**Once again, our
First Born led
the way.**

בְּבָנֵינוּ וּבִבְנוֹתֵנוּ בְּצֹאנֵנוּ וּבִבְקָרֵנוּ נֵלֵךְ

And Moses told the Pharoh, "We will all go.
We will go with our youth and our elders,
with our sons and our daughters with our
herds of sheep and cattle we will go." Exodus 10:9

וַיֹּאמֶר מֹשֶׁה בִּנְעָרֵינוּ
וּבִזְקֵנֵינוּ נֵלֵךְ

Let us now drink a FOURTH CUP OF WINE as we share our ancestors' joy in the fulfilment of Adonay's promise to bring us to a miraculous time—an era of a free Israel.

בָּרוּךְ אַתָּה יְיָ אֱלֹהֵינוּ מֶלֶךְ הָעוֹלָם בּוֹרֵא פְּרִי הַגָּפֶן.

Baruch ata Adonay Eloheynu melech ha-olam
  boray piree ha-ga-fayn.

Blessed are you Adonay our King, Creator of
the fruit of the vine.

NARRATOR: As our seder ends, we have studied our history and come to understand that the lamb shank symbolically recalls the pre-slavery Mount Horeb Festival of Adonay, and our animal sacrifices performed there. Our matzah too, always the sacred bread of firstborn and priests was eaten indoors during slavery, transforming those present into a Nation of Priests, responsible for carrying on the tradition of the Festival of Adonay. The bitter herbs, a medicine against the Ten Plagues, have reminded us of the danger to our health in the time just before the Exodus. So too we have thanked Adonay for teaching our elders dietary rules that miraculously spared our families. Today, many of us still observe the very same laws, such as shunning diseased animals or those that feed off unclean prey, describing them as unkosher.

חֲסַל סִדּוּר פֶּסַח כְּהִלְכָתוֹ כְּכָל מִשְׁפָּטוֹ וְחֻקָּתוֹ כַּאֲשֶׁר
זָכִינוּ לְסַדֵּר אוֹתוֹ כֵּן נִזְכֶּה לַעֲשׂוֹתוֹ

Cha-sal see-dur Pay-sach ki-heel-cha-to ki-chal meesh-pa-to
vi-chu-ka-to ka-asher za-cheenu li-sa-dayr oto kayn neez-keh
la-asoto.

The Pesach seder has now completed all requirements, according to
its rules and laws. As we have been privileged to share in our seder,
may we be privileged to do so again in the future.
Let us return to Zion with song!

לְשָׁנָה הַבָּאָה בִּירוּשָׁלָיִם

AND NOW FOR SOME SING-ALONG SONGS—the heart of our Pesach Heritage and tradition: Kee Lo Na-eh, Adir Hu, Echad Mi Yodaya, Had Gadya.

KEE LO NA-EH TO HIM PRAISE IS DUE

כִּי לוֹ נָאֶה

To Him praise is due. His faithful say of his awesome kingdom, while choosing to follow its laws--"To You Adonay belongs the Kingdom, To You all praise is due!"

Kee lo na-eh
kee lo ya-eh
Adir bimlu-cha ba-chur ka-ha-lacha
gidu-dav yom-ru lo

כִּי לוֹ נָאֶה
כִּי לוֹ יָאֶה
אַדִיר בִּמְלוּכָה בָּחוּר כַּהֲלָכָה
גְּדוּדָיו יֹאמְרוּ לוֹ

Le-cha u-lecha, lecha kee le-cha lecha af lecha lecha Adonay
ha-mam-lacha kee lo na-eh kee lo ya-eh (repeats as refrain)

לְךָ וּלְךָ
לְךָ כִּי לְךָ
לְךָ אַף לְךָ

לְךָ יְיָ הַמַּמְלָכָה כִּי לוֹ נָאֶה כִּי לוֹ יָאֶה

Dagul bimlu-cha hadur ka-ha-lacha va-teekav yom-ru lo

דָּגוּל בִּמְלוּכָה
הָדוּר כַּהֲלָכָה
וָתִיקָיו יֹאמְרוּ לוֹ

לְךָ וּלְךָ
לְךָ כִּי לְךָ
לְךָ אַף לְךָ

לְךָ יְיָ הַמַּמְלָכָה כִּי לוֹ נָאֶה כִּי לוֹ יָאֶה

Zakai bimlu-cha cha-seen ka-ha-lacha taf-srav yom-ru lo

זַכַּאי בִּמְלוּכָה
חָסִין כַּהֲלָכָה
טַפְסְרָיו יֹאמְרוּ לוֹ

לְךָ וּלְךָ
לְךָ כִּי לְךָ
לְךָ אַף לְךָ
לְךָ יְיָ הַמַּמְלָכָה כִּי לוֹ נָאֶה כִּי לוֹ יָאֶה

ADIR HU   MIGHTY IS HE

אַדִיר הוּא

Mighty, just, most high, He rules alone. He will build the Temple again. May He do so in our time in a place He chooses. Adonay build, build Your Temple soon.

Adir Hu, Adir Hu yiv-neh vay-to bi-karov bim-hayra bim-hayra bi-ya-maynu bi-karov

אַדִיר הוּא אַדִיר הוּא
יִבְנֶה בֵיתוֹ בְּקָרוֹב
בִּמְהֵרָה בִּמְהֵרָה
בְּיָמֵינוּ בְּקָרוֹב

אֵל בְּנֵה אֵל בְּנֵה
בְּנֵה בֵיתְךָ בְּקָרוֹב

El bi-nay El bi-nay Bi-nay vayt-cha bi-karov (repeats as refrain)

53

Ba-chur Hu gadol Hu da-gul Hu yiv-neh vayto bikarov
bim-hay-ra bim-hay-ra bi-ya-maynu bi-karov

בָּחוּר הוּא גָדוֹל הוּא דָגוּל הוּא
יִבְנֶה בֵיתוֹ בְּקָרוֹב
בִּמְהֵרָה בִּמְהֵרָה
בְּיָמֵינוּ בְּקָרוֹב

אֵל בְּנֵה אֵל בְּנֵה
בְּנֵה בֵיתְךָ בְּקָרוֹב

El bi-nay El bi-nay bi-nay vayt-cha bi-karov

Ha-dur Hu Va-teek Hu za-kye Hu yiv-neh vay-to bi-karov
bim-hay-ra bim-hay-ra bi-ya-maynu bi-karov

הָדוּר הוּא וָתִיק הוּא
זַכַּאי הוּא
בִּמְהֵרָה בִּמְהֵרָה בְּיָמֵינוּ בְּקָרוֹב

אֵל בְּנֵה אֵל בְּנֵה
בְּנֵה בֵיתְךָ בְּקָרוֹב

El bi-nay El bi-nay bi-nay vayt-cha bi-karov

Cha-seed Hu ta-hur Hu yacheed Hu yiv-neh vay-to bi-karov
bim-hay-ra bim-hay-ra bi-ya-maynu bi-karov

חָסִיד הוּא טָהוֹר הוּא יָחִיד הוּא
יִבְנֶה בֵיתוֹ בְּקָרוֹב
בִּמְהֵרָה בִּמְהֵרָה
בְּיָמֵינוּ בְּקָרוֹב

אֵל בְּנֵה אֵל בְּנֵה בְּנֵה בֵיתְךָ בְּקָרוֹב

54

אֶחָד מִי יוֹדֵעַ

Who knows One? I know One. One is Adonay, in the heavens and on earth. Who knows two? I know two. Two are the columns of the Ten Commandments. Who knows three? I know three. Three are the patriarchs (Abraham, Isaac and Jacob). Who knows four? I know four. Four are the matriarchs (Sarah, Rebeccah, Leah and Rachel). Who knows five? I know five. Five are the books of the Torah.

אֶחָד מִי יוֹדֵעַ אֶחָד אֲנִי יוֹדֵעַ
אֶחָד אֱלֹהֵינוּ שֶׁבַּשָּׁמַיִם וּבָאָרֶץ

Echad mee yo-day-ah echad anee yo-day-ah
echad Elo-haynu she-basha-my-eem u-va-arets

שְׁנַיִם מִי יוֹדֵעַ שְׁנַיִם אֲנִי יוֹדֵעַ
שְׁנֵי לֻחוֹת הַבְּרִית
אֶחָד אֱלֹהֵינוּ שֶׁבַּשָּׁמַיִם וּבָאָרֶץ

shi-ny-eem mee yo-day-ah shi-ny-eem anee yo-day-ah
shi-nay lu-chot ha-breet echad Elo-haynu
 she-basha-my-eem u-va-arets

שְׁלֹשָׁה מִי יוֹדֵעַ שְׁלוֹשָׁה אֲנִי יֹדֵעַ
שְׁלֹשָׁה אָבוֹת שְׁנֵי לֻחוֹת הַבְּרִית
אֶחָד אֱלֹהֵינוּ שֶׁבַּשָּׁמַיִם וּבָאָרֶץ

Shi-lo-sha mee yo-day-ah shi-lo-sha anee yo-day-ah
shi-lo-sha avot shi-nay lu-chot ha-breet
echad Elo-haynu she-basha-my-eem u-va-arets

אַרְבַּע מִי יוֹדֵעַ   אַרְבַּע אֲנִי יוֹדֵעַ
אַרְבַּע אִמָּהוֹת שְׁלֹשָׁה אָבוֹת
שְׁנֵי לְחוֹת הַבְּרִית אֶחָד אֱלֹהֵינוּ
שֶׁבַּשָּׁמַיִם וּבָאָרֶץ

Arba mee yo-day-ah arba anee yo-day-ah arba eema-hot
shi-lo-sha avot shi-nay lu-chot ha-breet
echad Elo-haynu she-basha-my-eem u-va-arets

חֲמִשָּׁה מִי יוֹדֵעַ חֲמִשָּׁה אֲנִי יוֹדֵעַ
חֲמִשָּׁה חֻמְשֵׁי תוֹרָה אַרְבַּע אִמָּהוֹת
שְׁלֹשָׁה אָבוֹת שְׁנֵי לְחוֹת הַבְּרִית
אֶחָד אֱלֹהֵינוּ שֶׁבַּשָּׁמַיִם וּבָאָרֶץ

Cha-mee-sha mee yo-day-ah cha-mee-sha anee yo-day-ah cha-mee-
sha chum-shay Torah arba eema-hot shi-lo-sha avot shi-nay lu-chot
ha-breet echad Elo-haynu she-basha-my-eem u-va-arets

CHAD GAD-YA   ONE BABY GOAT

חַד גַּדְיָא

One baby goat that Daddy bought for two coins. Along came a cat and
ate the goat. Then came a dog and bit the cat that ate the goat...and
along came a stick and hit the dog that bit the cat...and along came
fire that burned the stick that hit the dog...and along came water and
extinguished the fire that burned the stick...and then came an ox that
drank the water that burned the stick...and then came a butcher who
slaughtered the ox that drank the water that burned the stick...and
then came the angel of death who killed the butcher who slaughtered
the ox--and then came the Holy One, Blessed is He, who destroyed the
angel of death, who killed the butcher who slaughtered the ox that
drank the water that extinguished the fire that burned the stick that
hit the dog that bit the cat that ate the baby goat--that Daddy bought
for two coins.

חַד גַּדְיָא חַד גַּדְיָא דְּזַבֵּן אַבָּא בִּתְרֵי זוּזֵי
חַד גַּדְיָא חַד גַּדְיָא
וְאָתָא שׁוּנְרָא וְאָכַל לְגַּדְיָא דְּזַבֵּן אַבָּא בִּתְרֵי זוּזֵי
חַד גַּדְיָא חַד גַּדְיָא

Chad gad-ya chad gad-ya deez-van aba be-tray zu-zay
chad gad-ya chad gad-ya

וְאָתָא כַלְבָּא וְנָשַׁךְ לְשׁוּנְרָא דְּאָכַל לְגַדְיָא
דְּזַבַן אַבָּא בִּתְרֵי זוּזֵי
חַד גַּדְיָא חַד גַּדְיָא

vi-ata chal-ba vi-nashach li-shun-ra di-achal li-gad-ya
deez-van aba be-tray zu-zay
chad gad-ya chad gad-ya

וְאָתָא חוּטְרָא וְהִכָּה לְכַלְבָּא דְּנָשַׁךְ לְשׁוּנְרָא
דְּאָכַל לְגַדְיָא דְּזַבַן אַבָּא בִּתְרֵי זוּזֵי
חַד גַּדְיָא חַד גַּדְיָא

vi-ata chutra vi-he-ka li-chalba di-nashach li-shun-ra
di-achal li-gad-ya diz-van aba be-tray zu-zay
chad gad-ya chad gad-ya

וְאָתָא נוּרָא וְשָׂרַף לְחוּטְרָא דְּהִכָּה לְכַלְבָּא
דְּנָשַׁךְ לְשׁוּנְרָא דְּאָכַל לְגַדְיָא
דְּזַבַן אַבָּא בִּתְרֵי זוּזֵי
חַד גַּדְיָא חַד גַּדְיָא

vi-ata nura vi-saraf li-chutra di-he-kah li-chal-ba
di-nashach li-shun-ra di-achal li-gad-ya
deez-van aba be-tray zu-zay
chad gad-ya chad gad-ya

וְאָתָא מַיָּא וְכָבָה לְנוּרָא
וְאָתָא תוֹרָא וְשָׁתָה לְמַיָּא
חַד גַּדְיָא חַד גַּדְיָא

vi-ata ma-ya vi-cha-va li-nura vi-ata tora li-shata li-ma-ya
chad gad-ya chad gad-ya

וְאָתָא הַשּׁוֹחֵט וְשָׁחַט לְתוֹרָא
דְּשָׁתָה לְמַיָּא וְאָתָא מַלְאַךְ הַמָּוֶת וְשָׁחַת לְשׁוֹחֵט

57

דְשָׁחַט לְתוֹרָא דְשָׁתָה לְמַיָּא דְּכָבָה לְנוּרָא
דְּשָׂרַף לְחוּטְרָא דְהִכָּה לְכַלְבָּא
דְּנָשַׁךְ לְשׁוּנְרָא דְּאָכַל לְגַדְיָא
דְּאָכַל לְגַדְיָא
דְּזַבִּן אַבָּא בִּתְרֵי זוּזֵי
חַד גַּדְיָא חַד גַּדְיָא

vi-ata ha-sho-chayt visha-chat li-tora di-shata li-ma-ya
vi-ata ma-lach ha-mavet vi-shachat li-sho-chayt
di-shachat li-tora di-shata li-ma-ya di cha-va li-nu-ra
di-saraf li-chutra di-he-kah li-chal-ba di-nashach li-shun-ra
di-achal li-gad-ya
deez-van aba be-tray zu-zay
chad gad-ya chad gad-ya

וְאָתָא הַקָּדוֹשׁ בָּרוּךְ הוּא
וְשָׁחַט לְמַלְאַךְ הַמָּוֶת
דְשָׁחֵט לְשׁוֹחֵט דְשָׁחַט לְתוֹרָא
דְשָׁתָה לְמַיָּא דְּכָבָה לְנוּרָא
דְּשָׂרַף לְחוּטְרָא דְהִכָּה לְכַלְבָּא
דְּנָשַׁךְ לְשׁוּנְרָא דְּאָכַל לְגַדְיָא
דְּזַבִּן אַבָּא בִּתְרֵי זוּזֵי
חַד גַּדְיָא חַד גַּדְיָא

v-ata ha-kadosh baruch Hu
vi-shachat li-mal-ach ha-mavet
di-shacah li-sho-chayt
di sha-chat li-tora di shata li-ma-ya
di-chava li-nura di-saraf li-chut-ra
di-he-kah li chal-ba
di-nashach li-shunra di-achal li-gad-ya
deez-van aba be-tray zu-zay
chad gad-ya chad gad-ya

TO READ THE DISCUSSION WHICH FOLLOWS—
PLEASE TURN THE HAGGADAH 180 DEGREES.
THE ENGLISH MAY THEN BE READ IN ITS USUAL
LEFT TO RIGHT DIRECTION.

PASSOVER: TELLING IT LIKE IT WAS

For Starters...

The Passover holiday is a far more complicated subject than is generally recognized. In the following discussion, I shall begin with what most of us who have grown up in traditional homes have been taught.

The basic celebration of Passover—in Hebrew "Pesach"—begins at sundown of the 14th day of the Hebrew month of Nisan.

Actually, it starts the night before or that morning with a removing of the "Hamatz" (pronounced Cha-mayts). Hamatz means leaven and has come to mean anything leavened, or which may become leavened. What is leaven? Leaven is yeast, a variety of fungus, which acts on grain products in the presence of moisture to produce chemical changes. Upon coming in contact with flour, yeast produces tiny gas bubbles causing the flour to become porous and spongy—that is to rise. Such flour products (bread, cookies, crackers, pizza crust, bagels, pasta, pastries and cereal) are leavened. Varieties of liquids made from grain may undergo a similar process, more often called fermentation. Therefore grain vinegar, beer, and liquor made from grain are all Hamatz. Though many other food items are labelled "Kosher for Pesach," they are not halachically (legally) unkosher. For example, wine is not made from grain so it is not technically "unkosher for Pesach." The certification by a supervising authority simply guarantees that the wine and other such non-grain products did not come into contact with grain.

Sundown of the 14th of Nisan is the evening of the "seder," a festive mix of rituals, food, wine, prayers and song re-telling the story of the Hebrew escape from slavery in Egypt about 3,200 years ago. In Israel there is only one seder, elsewhere there are two (a custom owing to the uncertainty of lunar timing in the diaspora). The holiday lasts eight days.

Some key words and concepts:

Pesach: Pesach means to skip or "Pass over" and customarily refers to the moment in the story when the angel of death "passed over" Hebrew homes at the time of the tenth plague—when God struck down the first-born of every living Egyptian family, including livestock. Actually there is no angel of death mentioned in the Torah's version of the story. The Hebrew "Mashcheet" is more accurately the instrument or cause of death.

Seder: Seder literally means "order" and refers to the specific order of activities; rituals, telling the story, eating and saying prayers which are organized in a sequence of fifteen steps. Without listing them all (as they are summarized in the Haggadah), the rituals include "dipping twice"—greens into salt water, and bitter herbs into a sweet blend of apples nuts, raisins and honey—or other ingredients (recipes vary) which is called Haroset; as well as eating matzah, drinking wine—AND, taking a three-tiered plate of matzah, removing the middle piece, breaking it in half and hiding one part as the "Afikomen," to be eaten as the last food item (except for wine). Owing to its necessary ritual ingestion, the children hunt for it and blackmail the seder leader, demanding a gift, knowing he/she needs it to continue.

The Afikomen constitutes a symbolic return to the more spiritual side of the seder. The meal having been eaten, prayers are to follow, requiring a concentration on something other than the pleasant banter of a shared banquet.

Haggadah: After the afikomen is hidden (to back up a step), the "telling" of the Passover story commences. We call this segment of the seder "Maggid" and the book we use (from the same root) the "Haggadah"—both of which mean "Telling."

At the outset of the Maggid, an ancient tradition is to hold up a plate of matzah and invite all seder-less Jews to come in. No Jewish person may be excluded due to lack of family, funds, or friends. In ancient Jerusalem people actually went to their doorways and called out to possible "loners."

The words of the invitation, perhaps dating back 2500 years, are "Ha-lachma anya" which means "This is the bread of the poor" and continues: "Let all who are hungry come in and eat."

During the Maggid, which is based on the Torah, especially Exodus and Deuteronomy, little is said about Moses, at least by name. In fact, he is mentioned only once in most Haggadah versions. Though he is a hero, he is not THE hero. That is God. On Passover, as Maggid emphasizes, a true miracle occurs. God directly intervenes in history, and there is no room for any mistaken belief in the supposed powers of a human. (The story of Moses' being saved from the floating basket, killing an Egyptian taskmaster, fleeing to Midian, and being told by God at the burning bush to go to Pharoh and demand Hebrew freedom are not in most Haggadot—plural for Haggadah—but is found in the opening chapters of Exodus.)

Those of us who have joined in traditional seders are aware of a number of wonderful parts of the Maggid section.

Following the "invitation to the poor" the "Four Questions" are asked. This is customarily a children's event. (I guess adults are supposed to have all the answers.)

Often, the adults also ask, or join the children singing them in traditional tunes.

The questions ask why we are eating only unleavened bread (matzah), why we make such a big deal out of bitter herbs, why we dip twice, and why we sit in a reclining position (perhaps with a pillow, though they may have really leaned back on a different, setee-style chair two millenia ago).

The answers are not immediately stated in the Haggadah. Quite often, the answers are given by the children themselves who show off what they have already been taught. (Here, it is worth noting that an ancient rabbi, Gamaliel, said only three things MUST be explained. The matzah, lamb, and bitter herbs. I shall return to these three later.)

Two of the Four Questions (why dip and why bitter herbs) are the occasion to call attention to the "Seder Plate." On it, various ritual items are displayed: a green such as parsely, and salt water (the two items for the first dip), as well as bitter herbs (such as raddish), and haroset (the items required for the second dip), along with a roasted egg and a roasted lamb shank, which stimulate further commentary from the guests.

Standard answers are: We dip the green into salt water to taste the tears of slavery, and to anticipate the springtime of freedom. We dip the bitter herb (the bitterness of slavery), into the sweetness of freedom (haroset) for the same reason, more or less. The haroset is also said to symbolize the mortar used by the Hebrew slaves in their forced labor construction of Pithom and Ramses (large cities of the period).

Also on the seder plate, the roast lamb shank is meant to recall the final meal, the night of the escape from Egypt. On that night, the Torah tells us, there was a supper of roast lamb, and blood from the lamb was placed on the doorposts and lintels of every Hebrew home so death would Passover, causing the Hebrews no harm. Rabbis have compared it to the "outstretched arm of God" that saved the Hebrews. Personally the roast lamb shank never reminded me of God's arm.

No egg is mentioned in the Haggadah, but it may have found its way onto the seder plate as a symbol of birth— representing the birth of the Hebrew nation and new beginnings. It may also recall a second sacrifice offered as part of the ancient Temple service.

(Later, when I turn to the actual events of the original Passover night, I will re-visit the "final meal" eaten by the enslaved Hebrews prior to their escape.)

As for the matzah, it is explained as a symbol of our having to flee in such haste from Egypt that the bread did not have time to rise.

Often not a topic are the four cups of wine adult participants drink. Yet, they are significant. Each represents a phase in the process of escaping from bondage and reaching complete freedom. As one becomes intoxicated, the sense of being uninhibited and carefree is meant to elevate the festival's theme. In fact, each of us is meant to "make the journey" from the entrapment of difficult circumstances in our own lives to the new chance for a fresh start.

I would label them as follows: The Cup of breaking the

bonds, The Cup of courage to go forward, The Cup of growing confidence, the Cup of seeing God's promise to us fulfilled. (Note that they correspond exactly to escape from Egypt, crossing the desert, surviving the journey and reaching the Promised Land.)

After the Four questions have been asked and opinions exchanged about the various seder plate items, as well as explanation of the matzah, the seder proceeds.

One passage which stands out reads "Avadim ha-yinu"— WE were slaves... I actually had a student ask me why I always refer to the ancient Hebrews as "WE," when they lived long ago, and we are here now. I answered him that the word "we" joins us to them, defining our ancestors as our own family. Just as grandparents and parents leave an inheritance of values, of cultural and spiritual identity, we do the same—l'dor va dor, from generation to generation. And, in this spirit, we read, or sing, "We were slaves..."

This concept is continued in the next segment of Maggid, which concerns four different kinds of children—and the appropriate Passover lesson for each. The two who are most interesting are the "wise child" and the "wicked child." Their basic difference is that the wicked child says "You" in a scoffing tone when referring to the Hebrew family, excluding himself. (The Torah's specific instructions that a parent should teach the miracle did not happen to "them" but to "us" is generally quoted from Exodus 13:8 and Deuteronomy 6:23 in a passage read after Dayenu is sung, a little farther on.)

A song/prayer "V'hee She'amdah lavoteynu" continues the generational emphasis, stating that despite enemies in every generation God has saved us.

Maggid next contains passages from the Torah (Exodus and Deuteronomy) which tell of the circumstances of slavery in Egypt and God's saving the People. These are often read around the table by guests, taking turns.

After these readings, Maggid reaches the "Ten Plagues." As each is named, the participants dip a finger in their own wine cup and remove a drop, showing that there is no intention to rejoice over the misery of the Egyptians— that we are celebrating our freedom not their suffering.

Next we sing dayenu—The word "Dayenu" which means "It would have been enough for us" lists the separate miracles of our escape from Egypt. Though all of them were necessary, we sing of each, "it would have been enough." Perhaps, the idiom suggests each miracle was more than we could have hoped for—or, perhaps, there was meant to be humor in the reality that each alone would NOT have been enough. Either way, it's a fun song at the heart of our seder tradition. Following Dayenu, once again, the symbolism of the lamb, matzah and bitter herb are reiterated.

Next, two psalms are read, 113 and 114. This is the actual end of Part One of the seder. Part Two begins with the second cup of wine. It is the FOOD section. Hands are washed; Matzah, bitter herbs dipped in Haroset, and a bitter herb sandwich are eaten. By now, the meal is usually ravenously appreciated, as the starving guests dig in.

The final "food" event (see above) is the eating of the Afikomen. Birkat ha-mazon (thanking God for the food) is followed by drinking the third cup of wine and then opening the door for the prophet Elijah—and making sure his large wine cup is filled and visible to all. He is the prophet expected to usher in a new age of "fresh beginnings," even for those who have unworthy pasts. He is accorded the special role as a re-uniter of families and the one who will preside over the beginning of the messianic age when all mankind will live together in harmony.

Welcoming him, the participants sing, "Eliyahu ha-navi..." Elijah the prophet will come...

Here, it has become a custom to remember those who died in the Holocaust. Readings may be improvised.

Hallel (psalms 113-118) is completed and often psalm 115 is sung (y'varech et bayt yisrael...)

The fourth cup of wine is drunk.

Part Two comes to an end with the conclusion of the formal seder, "Nirtzah," which really means "completed in an acceptable form," or "as is acceptable." Several lines are read or sung emphasizing that the preceding ceremonies and rituals were done according to the Torah's requirements.

Part Three of the Seder is a musical sing-along. It begins with L'shanah ha-ba-ah Bee-rushalayim (Next Year in Jerusalem) and includes such favorites as:

Ki lo na-eh (To Him all Praise is due)
Adir Hu (Mighty is He)
Echad Mi yodaya (Who knows what one is?)
Chad Gadya (One kid)
And others which are the pleasure of the hosts (Eg. Jerusalem of Gold, Let My People Ago, Hatikvah...)

And Now for the actual Passover holiday, its historical background and origin.

First a few "facts"—more like strong possibilities. According to the Torah, Joseph was sold into slavery in Egypt by his brothers. After their reconciliation, when they purchased food from him in a time of drought and famine, their families all moved to Egypt and built a community in the area of Goshen, in the North-eastern Delta. That community was likely a magnet to a large number of Hebrews who took up residence in Egypt over an uncertain period of time—perhaps centuries.

After approximately four centuries (dating Joseph to 1,650 B.C.E.), there were about 1,000,000 Hebrews living there. At least, this is the number suggested by the Torah (Numbers 2:32).

The Pharoh who enslaved the Hebrews was most likely Ramses II (Ca. 1290-1213 B.C.E.) Exactly why Ramses II didn't like the Hebrews is uncertain. (Of course, we've been puzzled by hatred of our People so often, that it should not be surprising.) But there may be another cause of his decision to enslave the Hebrews besides simple contempt.

A possible lead in establishing Ramses II's motive for enslaving the Hebrews, is the prior "bad experience" with a People known as the Hyksos nation. The Hyksos were a Semitic people who invaded and conquered a part of Egypt in the mid-1700's B.C.E. Their expulsion in the 1500's B.C.E. from the same region that the Hebrews inhabited raises the possibility that they and the Hebrews dwelt together for a period of time. Their presence was considered hateful by the Egyptians—and if they were identified with the Hebrews as Semites, that contempt might have been spread to all Semites.

Adding to the liklihood that the dark days (for Egyptians) of Hyksos occupation caused contempt for all Semites, was the warfare between Egypt and Semites in Canaan. Seti I, who preceded Ramses II, as well as Ramses and his successor (a son) Merenptah, all faced major battles in their attempts to subdue Canaan. Their foes sometimes included the Apiru/Habiru, presumably Hebrews, who allied themselves with the local cities. Seti I mentions the Apiru in a victory stela from Beit She'an—and, Israel, as a nation is mentioned in about 1208 B.C.E. by Merenptah as subdued (the only such time the name occurs in Egyptian writing) at a site near the Sea of Galilee.

With so large a population of Hebrews living in Egypt, other Hebrews with whom the Pharohs had been doing battle in Canaan (obviously, therefore, not all Hebrews resided in Egypt), Ramses attitude might well have been that they constituted a genuine military threat—as had the Hyksos two centuries earlier. Exodus 1:10 supports this view. It quotes the Pharoh as saying, "Come let us outwit them (that is, the Hebrews) lest they multiply and in the event that we have war, they will join our enemies and fight against us..."

Though no hard evidence of the Exodus exists in Egyptian texts, or in Sinai wilderness finds of debris left by the Hebrews, there are explanations for that paucity. Rarely did Near Eastern palace chronicles record defeats (such as a rebellious people defying the Pharoh and quitting his dominion). And archeology may still discover traces of the Exodus, when the path the people travelled, including Mount Horeb/Sinai itself, are located with certainty. Archeology has excavated such storage cities as Pithom and Ramses, mentioned in the Torah (identified by the name Ramses on stone building blocks) and their mud-brick wall storage chambers may well have been built by the forced labor of Hebrews.

As for a description of Hebrew life and religion during the 400 years in Egypt (to be precise, 430 years according to Exodus 12:40), or the exact number of years of forced labor, the record is largely a blank.

In the following pages, I shall attempt to fill in the gap, providing a significant breakthrough in the area that concerns us here—Passover.

Because Egyptian records do not even mention Moses, or Hebrews living in Egypt, standard scholarship has attempted to "find" the Hebrews and illuminate their place in Egyptian history by examining victory inscriptions and wall paintings, and analyzing the historical references to Manetho, an ancient 3rd century B.C.E. Egyptian historian as he is quoted in Josephus.

My approach, which follows, begins with the premise that the Hebrews had been slaves between fifty and eighty years when the Passover escape-story occurs. The 50-80 year period is based on Moses' infancy occurring near the beginning of the oppression and his age at the time of the escape being between 50 and 70. (Exodus 7:7 says he was 80. Maybe. The desert journey is said to have lasted 40 years, and he dies at its conclusion at the age of 120.) These numbers may well be more the stuff of an accurate historical record than they first appear. Here's how: The Torah speaks of our slavery being mostly under one Pharoh—Exodus 2:23 (who dies just before the Burning Bush scene). Very likely, Moses returned to Egypt at the time of Ramses II's death—and actually was confronting the new Pharoh, his son Merenptah.

If Ramses II enslaved the Hebrews near the beginning of his rule (Ca. 1280 B.C.E.) and the escape took place not long after his death, under Merenptah (Ca. 1205) there is a match (75 years) between the two time-frames.

In any case there was not a long succession of Egyptian rulers during the period of Hebrew slavery. Having established a likely time-frame, I think it will be helpful to understand the overall viewpoint I shall be arguing in the following pages.

My thesis, in general terms, is this: Before the roughly 50-80 year period of forced labor began, the Hebrews celebrated an annual spring holiday called the "Festival (or Pilgrimage) of Adonay." It consisted of a three-day pilgrimage to a mountain called Horeb, one or two days of ceremonies at the mountain, and the three-day return trip.

The idea of such a pre-slavery Festival fits perfectly with the description of the exchange between Pharoh and Moses. Moses does not ask for complete freedom for the People—only that they be permitted to celebrate "the pilgrimage holiday of Adonay, " (Exodus 10:9) and that the People be permitted to make a three-day journey.

What holiday was he referring to?

Moses tells the Pharoh it is a "Festival to Adonay for all of us."

Thus we have a holiday that Moses himself is referring to as pre-escape. "It IS a Festival..." he says.

What kind of "Festival"? At the burning bush when God instructs Moses to go to the Pharoh (Exodus 3:18), he is told to tell the Egyptian king we must "perform a sacrifice to Adonay our God."

And, in Exodus 12:14-15 Moses tells the People: "This day (of escape) shall be a day of remembrance to you (to wit, the seder). You shall celebrate it as a Festival to Adonay...you must eat matzah for seven days..." The wording "pilgrimage/Festival of Adonay" is identical in both of Moses' references before the escape (Exodus 10:9) and, perhaps shortly after (Exodus 12:14).

These quotes suggest it was probably a holiday of national participation, with grain and animal sacrifices communally performed.

Furthermore, I propose, the pilgrimage was ritually supervised by elders and a "priesthood" of firstborn male Hebrews.

Harmless as it may sound to the lay-reader, the notion of such a priesthood is itself a serious revision of what has been a standard, traditional view that there was no such priestly stratum in the pre-Exodus period. The commonly accepted view is that that there could not have been priests because they were chosen later.

Those who were made priests after the escape, were chosen from the tribe of Levi, following their subduing the worshippers of the Golden Calf. (Rashi, commenting on Exodus 32:29 makes this assertion.)

But in Exodus 34:19 the first true clue to a pre-Exodus Hebrew priesthood of the firstborn males surfaces. We read:

(God said) "Every first issue of the womb is mine...." It is a statement of profound significance when linked to Numbers 3:11.

It reads:

"I hereby take the Levites from among the Israelites in place of all the firstborn...the Levites shall be Mine." So, the Levites are selected by God as substitutes for the firstborn males—expected to carry out those responsibilities, priestly ceremonies and sacrifices, which had been done by the firstborn. Following this change, the post-Exodus Levite priests had to be financially supported. With firstborn males available for full time work under the new scheme, families would be expected to bring an annual tax to the Levites, enabling them to perform their responsibilities without feduciary concerns.

Recognizing that a pre-Exodus priesthood of the firstborn males existed, I am not suggesting it was formed into a body-politic like the later priests—the Kohanim. No evidence of Hebrew shrines in pre-Exodus Egypt exists, nor am I suggesting there was a cult center over which a priestly corpus might preside.

On the contrary, the priesthood of the firstborn would have been active during the pilgrimage Festival of Adonay and in the home settings, leading the ritual observances with the household elders, the parents and grandparents.

Having made this distinction between the firstborn "priesthood" and later Levites, I again return to the notion of a pre-Slavery Hebrew pilgrimage holiday, one characterized by ceremony and ritual under the auspices of elders and firstborn males.

The holiday may well have been celebrated by sacrificing

and offering animals (goats, sheep, lambs) to Adonay, and making offerings of unleavened bread (matzah). During the celebration, the area(s) where the animals were killed and eaten was considered sacred—and kept absolutely pure, in the manner of cleanliness typical of what would later be the Mishkan (Temple–tent) and Temple. When the Hebrews were enslaved (circa 1280 B.C.E.), I propose, the pilgrimage was forbidden. As a result they moved the celebration into their own homes, and perhaps for as long as the 50-80 year period of slavery sacrificed their animals with gatherings of neighbors, transforming their houses into shrines with all the concomitant purity that had become tradition. The standards of hygiene and awareness of disease-causing impurity (detailed below) became the basis for a lifestyle which ultimately protected them from the devastation of the plagues. This "Festival of Adonay," having become a house-as-shrine event, I have re-named, calling it the "Nation of Priests" week. Perhaps those elders who happened to be firstborn, had continued to play a supervisory role, but all the people experienced a heightened sense of being equal in carrying out the requirements of the earlier pilgrimage to Horeb--especially because most firstborn males, being the fittest, had been taken away as slaves. (The male slaves probably ranged in age from 20-50). Therefore, those adults who were not conscripted into forced labor, functioned as firstborn/"priests" in the household performance of the Festival's rituals.

To suggest, as I am, that not all Hebrews were required to do forced labor, may seem to be at odds with the Torah's portrayal—but it is not. In Exodus 9:4 and 9:7 the Torah speaks of the "livestock of Israel" as not being affected by the plagues. In 10:9 Moses refers to the "flocks and herds" of the Hebrews. And, of course there is the fact that the Hebrews did have lambs to sacrifice on the last night. Even in Numbers 20:5 the reference to their lives in Egypt suggests they had "vines," as well as figs, grain and pomegranites. Arguably, the most striking evidence that slavery was not a state of complete destitution, are the post-Exodus contributions by the Israelites to the desert tabernacle. According to Exodus 35:22 they brought gold as well as precious objects.

Forced to move the ceremony into their own homes, sacrificing their salted lambs in open roasting pits outside the door, consecrating themselves to Adonay by holding up three different kinds of unleavened bread (detailed below), all participated in rituals which would later be taken over as those of the Levite "Kohanim." In the environment of homes transformed into shrines, many of what are today's seder rituals were actually institutionalized during the decades of the Nation of Priests' household ceremony. Some of our seder's rituals almost certainly have their origin in even earlier, pre-slavery times, dating to the Festival/pilgrimage of Adonay.

When the plagues struck, the Egyptians took note of the phenomenon that the Hebrews were not dying—while they, on the other hand, were. The belief that the Hebrew God was punishing them for the enslavement would have led to the attitude that the slaves should be let go.

(If this seems to make the enslavement into a "miracle in disguise," leading to purity-conscious lifestyles that saved us from the plagues, and paved the way for our freedom, I offer this thought: Without the enslavement, there would have been no overwhelming desire to get out of Egypt and return to Canaan, to eventually become the Hebrew Nation. Thanks to the plagues, the Egyptians were ultimately glad to get rid of us. But either way—with or without the plagues—slavery is what created the desire to escape. In fact, the Exodus without it is hard to imagine.) Keeping this thesis in mind, I think the facts may now be used to form a cogent argument for what actually occurred.

According to the Torah, the fateful night of escape was preceded by the repeated warnings of plagues, delivered to the Pharoh by Moses and Aaron. Repeatedly the Pharoh acquiesced, and then reversed his decision to let the Hebrews go, sometimes after the plague was lifted. (A theological note: Orthodoxy, in accepting the Torah's every word as historical, maintains the position that God literally refused to let the Pharoh let the Hebrews go and, as the Torah phrasing puts it, "hardened Pharoh's heart" after each plague so that the Divine power would be fully revealed through all ten. Those of us who emphasize other aspects of the Torah's account diminish the notion of a vengeful God, and have a different view.

Each plague, according to this more benificent approach, was intended to give the Pharoh another chance, rather than cause the Egyptians such devastation. This interpretation is consistent with our removing wine from our glasses each time a plague is mentioned. Also, it is worth noting that the Torah speaks of the Egyptians giving their gold jewelry to the escaping Hebrews. (Ex 11:3) Not all were happy about the Pharoh's enslavement policy— including his daughter who saved Moses—so applauding their suffering would be wrong. Finally, in Talmudic midrash it is said that God punishes the angels who rejoice over the death of the Egyptians. Hopefully we are all celebrating our freedom, not God's power to destroy.)

To gain an historical perspective, let's take a closer look at the 10 plagues.

Various scholars have noted a scientific basis for many of them. Generally, I subscribe to the view and summarize it as follows, supplying my own explanation of the 10th.

1. Blood: All bodies of water were turned to blood. If the "blood" was actually algae, known as the "red tide" by biologists, the oxygen would have been depleted from the various waterways. The red-tide algae proliferates in the sun and can even appear in mile-wide formations.

2. Frogs: Once the oxygen was depleted, fish would die, and frogs would emerge for air. Their need for shade would drive them to seek shelter in the Egyptian homes, and mounds of dead and dying frogs would have lined the shore.

3. Insects: Flies, lice, un-nameable bugs would have fed off the putrifying frogs. They would have landed everywhere in swarms.

4. Wild beasts: Hungry predators, looking for fresh water and food would have come closer to the populated areas. (Weakened herbivors, animals that relied on vegetation, such as goats, sheep, lambs and cows, might well have become easy prey.)

5. Cattle disease: The swarming, disease-carrying insects landed both on animals and people. The cattle would have developed external and internal diseases.

6. Boils: The people infected by the insects developed boils.

7. Hail: Not unheard of, a hailstorm in Egypt is still rare. If one occurred it would have probably been accompanied by darkness (the 9th plague).

8. Locusts: These huge flying insects are known as a plague in the Mideast, including Egypt. They sometimes occur in flying masses so immense and dense that they have the appearance of large clouds. When they land on the trees, fruit and grain, they can completely ruin the food supply.

9. Darkness: Which I place together with hail, number 7 above.

10. Death of the firstborn of Egyptians and their livestock. Given the Egyptian population was accustomed to eating meat, the death especially of the youngest individuals who ingested the diseased beef and lamb—or became terminally ill due to their contact with those who had touched the sick animals—is not surprising. Nor is the death of the young animals themselves.

Yet, the "firstborn" are generally not the youngest, but the oldest offspring. Here, the scientific overview appears to run into difficulty. I propose the following solution. Instead of "firstborn" let us say "first to be born after the plague started." This is especially likely because it parallels what the Pharoh did to the Hebrews in ordering the death of the male children "just being born."

Therefore, it would have been recognized as a plague, God's punishment taking the form of "an eye for an eye..." The fact that the 10th plague does not distinguish between firstborn males and females is evidence that it actually occurred. As a real plague, it would not have been gender-selective. But, why does the Torah say first-born—and not "first to be born after the plague started?"

The answer is that the text is implying the Divine intent to destroy the Egyptian gods. Standard generic dogma of Near Eastern religions was that the god was the chooser of those who would rule—that is, those who would inherit dominion over the earthly kingdom. And, the honor usually went to the firstborn—who might rule as kings, play priestly roles (like the firstborn Hebrews) or own vast tracts of land. To destroy the Egyptian first-born was therefore a statement of the Hebrew God's power to decide who would rule, and who would own the earth—eliminating the role of the Egyptian gods. It is revealing in this context to see that the decree of the death of the Egyptian firstborn is accompanied by the words, "I will mete out punishments to all the gods of Egypt, I the Lord." (Ex. 12:12)

Certainly, in an age of scepticism it helps to see that the plagues really happened. Nor is God's role diminished. Afterall, if God is the creator of nature, why shouldn't the plagues comply with those principles of nature created by God?

The next phase of this inquiry into the actual historical events of Passover requires that we broaden the approach. (The plagues and their role will not be fully set aside—but may now be placed in context.)

First, let's see what Passover was in its earliest form. (I refer to some passages of Torah detailing the period after the escape. Because one may question their relevance to the pre-Exodus lifestyle of Hebrews in Egypt, I shall show the link to earlier times.)

To uncover clues to the actual Passover history, we must first look closely at the "final meal" before the escape.

Exodus 12 begins by saying that God instructed Moses and Aaron concerning the final meal to be eaten in Egypt. Notably, the lamb to be slaughtered was to be selected four days before the fateful night, on the 10th of Nisan. Therefore, it was a dinner planned in advance.

At twilight the lamb was to be slaughtered by the entire People, and eaten by groups of Israelites in their own homes, or in the homes of neighbors. Sundown of the 14th day of Nisan began the dinner. According to Exodus 12:8 the meal was to include three obligatory foods: 1. Roast lamb, cooked over fire (not boiled or stewed) 2. Unleavened bread (matzah) and 3. Bitter herbs. (The mention of these three was therefore considered necessary by Gamliel, as noted earlier).

For our purpose, the most striking of the three items is the unleavened bread. Afterall, the reason we are supposedly eating matzah is to recall the haste of the escape when the bread did not have time to rise. But with four days of planning, the meal could certainly have had leavened bread without rushing. Moreover, the Hebrews could hardly have been recalling something that had not yet happened.

So why unleavened bread?

In fact, immediately after the escape, when the Mishkan (the desert Temple-tent) was built, the matzah was of fundamental importance to the priesthood as an especially necessary part of their ritual foods and ceremonies. Indeed, it was a bread of holiness having nothing to do with the escape from Egypt.

Here is a revealing passage concerning ritual use of unleavened bread by the priests:

"Every meal offering that you (the priests) bring to the Lord shall be free of leaven. For no leaven...may be caused to smoke as an offering...to the Lord." Levit. 2:11-12

The Torah's recipe for unleavened bread is for three types: baked unleavened cakes with oil mixed in; baked unleavened wafers spread with oil, and pan-fried flour mixed with oil. Levit. 2:4-7

In Exodus 29:1-29:2 the ceremony of consecrating Aaron's sons to serve as priests uses the three types:

"Take....unleavened bread, unleavened cakes mixed with oil, and unleavened wafers thinly covered with oil...place these in one basket and present them..."

Is that because such bread was a memorial of the hasty escape from Egypt? Clearly the answer is no. And, no such symbolism is stated at the consecration ceremony.

In this instance, the pure leaven-free bread functioned solely as a ritual component of the priestly consecration event.

In recognizing the role of matzah in priestly consecration, we may now make the first serious surmise concerning the purpose of the matzah at the final dinner. The matzah was eaten as a sign we were all acting as a Nation of Priests.

Very likely it was originally the bread of consecration of the firstborn into their "priestly" status, at the age they were mature enough to accept such a role. At Mount Horeb, in the days of the pre-slavery pilgrimage, the three types of matzah may have been a food also eaten by all the People, consecrating everybody to God, as a Nation of Priests. My view is that all the kinds of matzah were eaten by everybody in those pre-slavery generations— when it was called a "Pilgrimage/Festival of Adonay" (as noted above).

The special role of the firstborn may, however, have been dramatized by their offering the three types of unleavened bread at the fire pits where the lambs were roasted. The physical act of "offering" the breads would have been to hold up each type on the palms of their hands, in an elevated manner and then to put them into the fire to be totally consumed. (Exodus 29:23-25). (A slight variation is suggested in Leviticus 6:7—but is a manner of meal-offering not associated with priestly consecration).

As a household ceremony during the period of slavery, with everybody eligible—not just the elders—to elevate and eat the three matzot, the Nation of Priests was fully manifest.

Exodus 19:6 puts the national consecration concept into words. God says, "...you shall be to me a Kingdom of Priests and a holy nation. These words you shall speak to the Children of Israel."

Equally, the Divine edict of a Nation of Priests is rendered in Exodus 4:22: "Thus says the Lord—'Israel is my Firstborn son (among the nations)'"

As I have noted above, the firstborn were considered the priestly performers of ritual—and so, the parallel is analagous, that the Firstborn nation was a priestly nation.

83

Furthermore the three pieces of matzah today displayed on every traditional seder table very likely has its origin in a consecration of firstborn-as-priests ceremony beginning in pre-slavery Egypt, carried on as a national consecration in the household celebration (during slavery), and continued as described in Exodus 29:1 once the new priests of Levi took over from the firstborn. (The standard interpretation is that the three matzot represent the priests, Levites and Israelites. I believe we may now recognize this to be a later explanation.)

(NOTE: Scholars have long observed that there was another holiday, the "matzah-holiday" which was combined with our Passover holiday. The fact is we even find its name, "Hag ha-Matzot," in the Torah, for example Exodus 34:18. Yet, not much more has been said about it and it has been generally considered an "artifact" of a spring harvest celebration.)

To understand the holiness of unleavened bread, and how it earned its role in the priests' consecration, and in the consecration of the whole People as a Nation of Priests—we must understand the nature of its purity.

Leavened bread was fluffy or spongy because its flour had interacted with yeast, a variety of fungus. (As noted earlier, small gas bubbles cause the fluffiness that makes the bread rise).

Similar interactions with other substances had produced apparent contamination. Mildew was recognized as a contamination, as was flaking skin—including the symptom of the dread disease leprosy.

Here is a remarkable selection of post-Exodus passages from Leviticus 14:34—14:47 which reveal the connection between mildew and disease—ultimately related to unleavened bread and purity.

"When you reach the Land of Canaan...and I inflict an eruptive plague upon (one of your) houses...the owner shall tell the priest, 'there's something that looks like plague in my house...'"

"If when he (i.e. the priest) examines the plague in the walls of the house, with the walls having greenish or reddish streaks that appear to be deep, the priest shall...close the house for seven days." And—"Whoever sleeps in the house must wash his clothes, and whoever eats in the house must wash his clothes...if the plague has spread in the house...the house is unclean...the house shall be torn down."

Even if leavened bread was not a cause of illness, its flour had been infiltrated and caused to change in a similar fashion to contamination of damp walls (mildew). Most likely the connection was made owing to the smell of mildew, and the green spots that may form on old leavened bread.

(Note: Bread that was leavened could also be considered pure—but it could not be offered on the altar. The distinction is made in Levit. 2:12—2:13, and the pure leavened bread is indicated in Levit. 23:17; 24:5).

These passages (and many others not quoted here) illustrate the legacy of pre-Exodus priestly precepts taken over by Levite priests in their role as examiner, evaluator of disease-causing impurities, and as "separator" of the pure from the impure. Purity was therefore the guarantor of Life just as impurity shared the properties of possible illness and death.

Conforming to the same laws that prohibited the sacrifice of maimed or sick animals to God, leavened bread could not be burned as the "grain/meal" or "mincha" offering.

As the future overseers of such rituals, the newly consecrated priests ceremonially emphasized the significance of unleavened bread, thus accepting the responsibility for keeping the shrine separate from all contamination.

Having established matzah as the bread of priestly consecration, here are two more matzah-related Nation of Priests rituals which have found their way to our own seder tables:

1. On the night or morning before the Passover, it is customary to search and clean the house, purifying it of all Hamatz. The morning search for impurities and leftovers or contaminated food, was standard daily activity of the priests.

2. At our seder, the plate of matzah is held aloft (during the invitation to the poor) imitating the priests holding the offering of unleavened bread aloft.

(No evidence exists that these were pre-escape rituals, but the more strongly we link our seder to the pre-Exodus household Nation of Priests celebration, the more likely that becomes. Though some will argue that the pre-escape meal was a later literary invention serving to institutionalize the seder, the matzah at that meal was incompatible with the seder's "institutional" symbolism of a hasty departure. Moreover, putting blood on the doorposts was not institutionalized as something one should do at the seder.)

Naturally, my assertion that our seder is re-enacting a pre-Exodus "Nation of Priests" week requires more than eating the same unleavened bread as the priests. As I proceed, I will show that the pre-Exodus final meal (the night of the escape) as well as our own entire seder is filled with an acting out of priests' rituals—and that these were mostly associated with purity standards that were meant to ward off plague. (Given the historical reality of the Ten Plagues, the anti-plague rituals probably were introduced when the devastation began toward the end of the period of slavery. I shall consider them in turn.)

First, let's see what the lamb sacrifice was all about. As a ritual it was part of the Festival of Adonay (the pre-slavery pilgrimage). And, it was part of the household Nation of Priests celebration, carrying on the earlier tradition. After the Exodus, the lamb sacrifice was a national participation event. At our own seder, it is memorialized by a lamb shank on the seder plate.

The lamb sacrifice: The sacrifice of all animals from the earliest post-escape period was to be performed only by the priests. The only exception was Passover.

The prevailing view holds that Torah law dictates national participation (Exodus 12:3) and therefore everybody, not only the priests, sacrificed their lambs. Yet, the point of such national involvment has been lost. Most important was not the sharing of the Festival per se, as is the general perception, but was the transformation of the People into a national priesthood.

Placing blood on the doorways of the houses, as attested at the final pre-escape meal, appears to also stem from the community acting as a nation of priests.

Familiar to most of us, is the dramatic commandment to take the blood of the lamb sacrificed that fateful night, and to put it on the doorposts and lintels of each home (so God would see it and have the deliverer of death Pass over on the way to smiting the Egyptian firstborn—the 10th plague).

"And all the congregation...shall take some of the blood and put it on the two doorposts..." Exodus 12:6-7

In fact, one of the most strongly emphasized post-Exodus rituals the priests performed after any sacrifice of an animal was to take its blood and sprinkle it around the shrine.

Therefore, we can add blood-sprinkling to the list of rituals which defined the holiday as a Nation of Priests week.

No matter in what manner, or on what occasion, the sprinkling was based on a unified concept, illustrated by various post-Exodus passages:

"Aaron came forward to the altar and slaughtered his...offering. Aaron's sons brought the blood to him; he dipped his fingers in the blood and put it on the horns of the altar...and he threw (the blood) on all surfaces of the altar..." (Leviticus 9:8-9, and 9:12)

In other passages, the blood is described as having the power to atone for sin and to cleanse the shrine of uncleanness and sin. (Levit. 16:16)

The blood might also be sprinkled around the innermost part of the shrine (the Holy of Holies) on what we have come to call Yom Kippur.

Why did the priests do this? The blood was thought to contain the power of life. (Early observers had undoubtedly realized that whatever the red, sticky stuff was, when enough of it came out of you or an animal, death followed.) Because God was the source of life—and the vanquisher of death—it followed that the substance containing God's essential power of life would prevent the forces of death from entering the precinct of the shrine. Malevolent forces would certainly Pass- over rather than infiltrate the area which was sanctified by God's power of life in the form of blood.

Sometimes blood was used as an antidote to illness and plague. It was, in these instances always the priests who performed the lustration.

Because it was an anti-plague ritual, and was the one which occurred the night of the escape, it warrants special attention:

Leviticus 14:51 describes the "treatment" which I am quoting only as an exerpt:

"(The priest) shall take the...hyssop and dip it in the blood (of a bird)...and sprinkle it on the house..."

Thus the house was purged of all illness and plague by putting blood on it! Those who applied the blood to the doorposts and lintels at the last meal on Passover, were performing an anti-plague ritual. But they were doing it on the doorway of the house-as-shrine, not using a bird's blood. Thus it melds the rite of ritual blood lustration after a sacrifice with an anti-plague function. Like the eating of the unleavened bread, this act appears to have become a basic component of the Nation of Priests week. Yet, it is specifically connected with plague. Therefore, one may infer that it was likely added to the Nation of Priests holiday in the time of the Ten Plagues. (Perhaps a bird's blood was used up until the fateful night, when the last meal involved using the lamb's blood, as the Torah states.)

Having asserted that the blood on the doorway at the final meal before escape had a particular anti-plague purpose (as the Torah rendition suggests), I now will discuss the modern seder's two "dips."

Scholars have observed that our seder's first dip (parsely into saltwater) actually was standard at Hellenistic and Roman meals, when greens were dipped in salad dressing as an appetizer. And, the point is well taken. The Talmudic version of the Four Questions even asks "Why on all other nights do we dip only once, while on this night we dip twice?"

But once again, I believe we must search earlier tradition to discover the actual origin of the first dip—an origin having nothing to do with dipping greens into salad dressing.

We may recognize the original "Karpas Dip," identifying its intent from a passage in Numbers 19:14-19:20.

Here is the description: "When a person dies in a tent, whoever enters the tent and whoever is in the tent shall be unclean seven days. Every open vessel with no lid fastened down shall be unclean. And in the open, anyone who touches a person who was killed, or who died naturally...or the grave shall be unclean seven days....A person who is clean shall take hyssop, dip it in water, and sprinkle on the tent and on all the people who were there (and came into contact with the corpse).

I believe that in the period of the Ten Plagues, people were using this form of lustration to ceremonially purify each other. Whether or not we have direct evidence of this water-cleansing dip the fateful night of escape (and we do not), it is an anti-plague dip that is present immediately after the escape. Therefore, it is no stretch to infer that even if it was not done at the final meal—it may well have been part of a constellation of pre-escape purification rituals used to ward off the Ten Plagues.

And, a word about the salt water that is an ingredient of our Karpas dip. As the Torah instructs (Leviticus 2:13), no offering could be placed on the altar unless it had been salted (probably because its power to keep food from spoiling earned it a special status as a purifying ingredient to prevent shrine contamination). Its inclusion in the water of our first dip may owe itself to this ritual importance. Perhaps it is a fairly recent addition, occurring when the lamb was no longer sacrificed and salted. If so the salt was mixed with the water as a dipping component after the destruction of the Temple.

Now let us consider the second dip, bitter herbs into haroset.

Bitter herbs were never part of a priestly ritual. As a reminder of the bitterness of slavery, the Torah says nothing. Then what were they? I strongly suspect they were medicinal, just as bitters are still used for intestinal and digestive maladies. They too functioned as a plague-deterrent, in the form of a food that had God's curative powers to keep away plague. Dipping them into something sweet (haroset) would have made the "bitter medicine" more palatable, especially to the children.

Though the final Passover meal does not mention any

such dip at all, I strongly suspect it was part of the standard supper during the plagues—and bitter herbs were likely to have been dipped into haroset to make them more edible at the last meal before escape.

Admittedly the search for an ancient precedent to our seder's dipping rituals is speculative. The hyssop-in-blood and hyssop-in-water as well as the bitter herbs eaten at the last pre-escape meal are nonetheless important evidence of historical realities. They prove that the Hebrews were extremely aware of plague and conscious of contagion during the critical period of the Exodus.

Now, I shall argue the all-important view that the Hebrews did not get sick from the Ten Plagues—that early dietary and hygienic standards, later to be codified as "ablution" and "kosher" laws—prevented their contracting them. (If the Hebrews actually seemed immune to the Ten Plagues the Egyptians would almost certainly ascribe their suffering to the Hebrew God. Indeed, they would have perceived the Hebrew God as having brought the plagues upon them.)

Before looking for evidence that the Hebrews living in Egypt were especially conscious of an animal's physical condition, and were guarding their homes from contamination and the spread of contagion, via disease-carrying insects, or sick cattle, let's have a look at the earliest post-escape texts. I think the following quotes are informative:

"No (priest) who has a (skin) eruption shall eat the (offering)." Levit. 22:4

"If a (priest) touches anything contaminated by a corpse...or touches any swarming thing by which he is made unclean or any human being by whom he is made unclean...he shall not eat unless he has washed his body in water...he shall not eat anything that has died or been torn by beasts, thereby becoming unclean..." Levit. 22:4-22:8

Further:

"(An animal offered as a sacrifice) must be without blemish...anything blind or injured or disfigured...with a boil-scar or scurvy (you shall not offer as a sacrifice). Levit. 22:21-22:22

And:

"When you sacrifice...it shall be eaten on that day. You shall not keep any of it until morning." Levit. 22:30

Keeping these ritual laws in mind, the question is: do they refer only to later priestly purity, or were they in force during the pre-Exodus period of the Ten Plagues?

The answer is that there is a startling match between the early post-Exodus ritual purity requirements and the Ten Plagues, indicating the requirements were designed to ward off the illnesses that had struck down the Egyptians.

To wit:

Plague number three (contagion carried by insects) is prevented by "not touching any swarming thing."

Plague number four (wild beasts and putrifying animals killed by them) is thwarted by "not eating anything that has been torn by beasts."

Plague number five (cattle disease—with the symptoms of skin disease and scarring) is matched by not eating any animals "blemished, or with scars or scurvy."

Plague number six (boils on people) is handled by the requirement that no person making an offering may do so if they have a skin eruption.

The death of the "first to be born" (the most vulnerable) after the onset of the other plagues, was a consequence of parents, family, nursemaids, or servants touching, or eating, animals that had become sick, or had died and spreading disease to the young. As quoted above, it was prohibited to eat anything that had died (a natural death, and was therefore sick, or putrifying)—or to eat after touching a corpse (a common problem with mass deaths due to plague.)

The injunction "it shall be eaten in the same day...you shall not leave any of it to morning" is an instruction identical to the time of the pre-escape meal, Exodus 12:10.

As an anti-plague hygienic chore, removing the leftovers would have prevented contamination of the eating environment by food waste.

Here, though I hesitate to add anything to the puzzle, one must raise another question. Since they would all hurriedly make their escape at midnight, one may wonder what difference it made whether they left behind uneaten food (rather than burn it). And, how was it they were told "Don't keep/leave anything until 'morning' "? If they were gone at midnight, they wouldn't be there in the morning.

My impression is that the rule of "cleaning up before morning" was codified long BEFORE the evening of the escape, and was a regulation dating to the pre-slavery period of the Festival of Adonay, and certainly to the period of the plagues.

In fact, this brings us to what will hopefully be a clarifying look at the description of that last meal. It has two main ritual aspects: One involved all participants performing as a Nation of firstborn/priests (re-living the Festival of Adonay, before enslavement) and the other was dealing with plague.

Under the heading "Nation of Priests" components, having the Festival of Adonay as its antecedent, I place:

A. Examining and selecting a lamb for sacrifice
B. Sacrificing a lamb
C. Roasting the lamb over fire (mimicking the flames of a sacrificial site or altar)
D. Putting its blood on the doorway, emulating the altar or roasting pits at Mount Horeb (this was also anti-plague)
E. Eating matzah

These are all attested in Exodus 12.

I believe the following Nation of Priests rituals may also have been in place at the time of the final meal. They are based on relics that are found in our own Passover and seder observance:

F. Searching for and removing Hamatz .
G. Elevating the matzah
H. Displaying and using a three-tiered basket of unleavened bread

Under the heading "Anti-plague" components, I place:

A. Examining the selected lamb for FOUR days prior to sacrifice
B. Putting blood on the doorway
C. Eating bitter herbs
D. Thoroughly roasting the lamb—so as not to eat any of it raw

These are all attested in Exodus 12.

I also include the following list of anti-plague activities which may have been part of the Ten-Plague regimen. These are based on codified norms following the escape:

E. Washing one's body and one's hands
F. Dipping a green into water and sprinkling it on one to be cleansed of contamination.

As I have suggested, various of these components likely arose in the period of the Ten Plagues. By turning each home into a virtual Temple—purified and sanctified— the protection from plague would have been much greater. God would be protecting the house.

Closing comments:

If what I have argued is true, the thesis should solve several perplexing questions.

The People who escaped, we are informed (Exodus 12:39) ate unleavened bread after they got out because the bread did not have time to rise.

We have already seen that matzah was actually the ritual

bread of priestly consecration. With four days to prepare for the meal, eating it had nothing to do with a hurried escape. But the question remains as to why it was eaten during and immediately after the departure from Egypt.

The answer is surprisingly simple: The established tradition, as stated in the Torah, to eat it for seven days (Ex. 12:15) was likely based on the time it had always taken the People (pre-slavery) to make their pilgrimage to Horeb: 3 days travelling, 1 day of sacrifice and ceremony at the mountain, and 3 days to return. Therefore, if the escape from Egypt, and the final meal, took place at the beginning of the 7-day period, they would be in the middle of the 7-day period during their escape! The people ate matzah because the escape happened at the outset of the seven-day holiday.

Equally suggestive of an ongoing long-celebrated "Festival of Adonay," is the how-to when it came to making their homes into miniature temples. It seems impossible that out of nowhere, the average householder improvised unleavened bread, suddenly decided to perform a Passover lamb sacrifice according to priestly rules, and transformed the home into a shrine.

Is it possible, for example, that someone attempting to prevent being struck by the 10th Plague said, "I have a good idea—let's put blood on the doorway!" Or, "OK everybody—no more leavened bread!"

Yet these are exactly the things that are described as components of the final meal—and without any acknowledged precedents.

(If I seem to be setting aside the Torah's description that these were performed in obedience to God's commandments to Moses—I admit to having adjusted the origin of the rituals, placing them in a pre-Moses period. Of course they may have found increased resonance during the period of slavery and ultimately the time of the Ten Plagues.)

Incontrovertibly, the Nation of Priests holiday was extant in Egypt long before that fateful night of departure.

But what about the anti-plague components? When did they originate? I think they would have very naturally become part of the indoor holiday during the period of the Ten Plagues. Afterall, the firstborn/priests were the main delineators of pure from impure—a pre-condition to removing dangerous contaminants.

In this context, one may again note the four-day period between the selection of the lamb and its sacrifice. Rashi and other rabbinic commentaries point out that only in Egypt was the Passover sacrificial lamb purchased four days early.

In the environment of blight on the animals, and the threat of contagion, during the Ten Plagues the four-day examination seems a logical precaution. Subsequently (Mechilta, Pesachim 96a), a four-day period of examination of the Passover lambs became customary.

Based on this observation, we can surmise that many of the hygiene laws, and dietary regulations may well have originated in Egypt before the escape.

It is no wonder that Hebrews had a religious tradition of dietary and household purity. Such was the legacy of the Festival of Adonay, institutionalized during slavery, and certainly emphasized during the period of the Ten

Plagues. Refusing to eat with unwashed neighbors, or to touch food after contact with diseased animals or people—or their corpses—the Hebrew people had defacto protected themselves against the Ten Plagues.

In other words it was the hygienic rituals and dietary laws (the word kosher was not used until the Talmudic period) that saved the Hebrews from the Ten Plagues. No wonder the purity laws were understood to be commandments from God!

Rejecting the meat of sick or dead animals, prohibiting the eating of animals that might have fed off other animals (pigs eat rats, shellfish eat everything, predatory birds and beasts feed off putrifying carcasses) saved their lives.

Of further interest are the post-Exodus dietary laws prohibiting shellfish and scale-less bottom-feeders. Almost certainly, the polluted waters added to their toxicity, as these kinds of sea-life ingested sick and dead fish matter. With food having become scarce, owing to hailstorms and locusts (the Torah says these plagues destroyed the crops), one imagines the near-starved Egyptians catching crabs and clams, and perhaps eels in the slimy red waters—while the Hebrews avoided them.

If our dietary restraints against shellfish began before the plagues, as may be the case, they must have gained the stature of divine prohibitions, life-saving commandments, when the waters turned putrid.

Having saved everybody, the purity laws were understood to be laws inspired by God, to be observed as sacred for all time. Today, as we know, Jews often adopt new scientific standards to determine the safety of food-stuffs, giving less weight to the Torah's description of clean and unclean. To many, keeping kosher is a way of remembering and being thankful for God's miracles.

In summing up:

The purity-conscious lifestyles of the enslaved People, ritualized in washing, examining animals and each other for uncleaness or disease, heightened by ceremonial ablutions and lustrations with water and blood, probably were traditions dating to the Festival of Adonay long before Hebrew enslavement.

In the period of slavery, foods would be closely scrutinized and rituals more carefully performed so that Adonay would hear their prayers for freedom to make the three-day pilgrimage to Horeb. One detail worth noting is the instruction concerning the clothing to be worn during the last meal. "This is how you shall eat it. Your loins girded, your sandals on your feet and your staff in your hand." Exodus 12:11 More than likely they ate in this fashion the entire fifty-to-eighty years of the indoor celebration praying for their freedom, and showing God they would be ready for the pilgrimage to His Mountain, Horeb.

Even the four-day advance selection of a sacrificial lamb may have originated with the pilgrimage holiday—rather than a hygienic period of examination. If the People usually set out on the 11th of Nisan, in order to reach the mountain by the 14th, they would have needed to acquire their animals ahead of time. Having done so for generations, the enslaved Hebrews may have wished God to see they were prepared to make His pilgrimage once they were free.

Finally, when the plagues struck and Hebrew homes were spared, many Egyptians thought they were being punished by the Hebrew God.

God could not have constructed the miracle of our escape in any more formidable or believable manner.

As I conclude this discussion, it is with a Hebrew toast: Lehayim! Our blessing over the fruit of the vine reminds us that when the waters of Egypt became poisonous, Adonay sustained us with the juice of grapes. And, yes, I suspect that is the origin of our kiddush, giving special meaning to its phrase: "zaycher letsiyat Mitsrayim..." that the wine is a sacred reminder of surviving the plagues upon Egypt.

If I have awakened a memory of a time of equality of all our People before God, then these words and thoughts have been worthwhile. A nation of priests is a nation of equals. No person should feel he or she is less worthy than any other at our seder, or at other times. The Nation of Priests holiday is alive and well at our own seder and during our own Passover holiday so long as this idea binds us all: None of us should pass judgment on what God finds acceptable as personal offerings from fellow Jews. We are all the priests of our tradition, heritage and commandments.